THE WATER MIRROR

THE WATER MIRROR

KAI MEYER

TRANSLATED BY ELIZABETH D. CRAWFORD

MARGARET K. MCELDERRY BOOKS
NEW YORK   LONDON   TORONTO   SYDNEY

Margaret K. McElderry Books
An imprint of Simon & Schuster Children's Publishing Division
1230 Avenue of the Americas, New York, New York 10020

English language translation copyright © 2005 by Elizabeth D. Crawford
Die Fliebende Koenigin: Text © 2001 Kai Meyer
Original German edition © 2001 Loewe Verlag GmbH, Bindlach

Published by arrangement with Loewe Verlag

First U.S. edition, 2005

Book design by Ann Zeak
The text for this book is set in Stempel Garamond.
Manufactured in the United States of America
2 4 6 8 10 9 7 5 3 1
CIP data for this book is available from
the Library of Congress.
ISBN-13: 978-0-689-87787-2
ISBN-10: 0-689-87787-0

Contents

1

MERMAIDS

THE GONDOLA CARRYING THE TWO GIRLS EMERGED FROM one of the side canals. They had to wait for the boats racing on the Grand Canal to pass, and even then, for minutes afterward there was such a jumble of small rowboats and steamboats that the gondolier chose to wait patiently.

"They'll be past pretty soon," he called to the girls as he grasped his oar with both hands. "You aren't in a hurry, are you?"

"No," replied Merle, who was the older of the two. But actually she was more excited than she'd ever been in her life.

People in Venice had been talking about nothing but the regatta on the Grand Canal for days. The promoters had advertised that the boats would be drawn by more mermaids at once than ever before.

Some people disparaged the mermaids as "fishwives." That was only one of the countless abusive terms they used for them, and worst of all was the claim that they were in league with the Egyptians. Not that anyone seriously believed such nonsense—after all, the armies of the Pharaoh had wiped out untold numbers of mermaids in the Mediterranean.

In today's regatta there were to be ten boats at the starting line, at the southern end of the Grand Canal, at the level of the Casa Stecchini. Each would be pulled by ten mermaids.

Ten mermaids! That had to be an all-time record. *La Serenissima*, most serene lady, as the Venetians liked to call their city, had never seen anything like it.

The mermaids were harnessed in a fan shape in front of the boats on long ropes that could withstand even needle-sharp mermaid teeth. The people were gathered to watch the show on the right and left sides of the canal wherever its banks were accessible and, of course, on all the balconies and in the windows of the palazzos.

But Merle's excitement had nothing to do with the regatta. She had another reason. A better one, she thought.

The gondolier waited another two or three minutes

before he steered the slender black gondola out into the Grand Canal, straight across it, and into the opening of a smaller canal opposite. As they crossed, they were almost rammed by some show-offs who'd harnessed their own mermaids in front of their boat and, bawling loudly, were trying to act as if they were part of the regatta.

Merle smoothed back her long, dark hair. The wind was making her eyes tear. She was fourteen years old, not big, not small, but a little on the thin side. That was true of almost all the children in the orphanage, though, except of course for fat Ruggiero, but he was sick—at least that's what the attendant said. But was it really a sign of illness to sneak into the kitchen at night and eat up the dessert that was to be for everyone else?

Merle took a deep breath. The sight of the captive mermaids made her sad. They had the upper bodies of humans, with the light, smooth skin that many women probably prayed for every night. Their hair was long, for among the women of the sea it was considered shameful to cut it off—to such an extent that even their human masters respected this custom.

What differentiated the mermaids from ordinary women was, for one thing, their mighty fish tails. The tails began at the level of their hips and were rarely shorter than six and a half feet. They were as agile as whips, as strong as lions, and as silvery as the jewelry in the treasury of the City Council.

But the second big difference—and it was the one that humans feared most—was the hideous mouth that split a mermaid's face like a gaping wound. Even though the rest of their features might be human, and strikingly beautiful as well—innumerable poems had been written about their eyes, and not a few love-smitten youths had voluntarily gone to a watery grave for them—still it was their mouths that convinced so many that they were dealing with animals and not with humans. The maw of a mermaid reached from one ear to the other, and when she opened it, it was as if her entire skull split in two. Arising from her jawbone were several rows of sharp teeth, as small and pointed as nails of ivory. Anyone who thought there was no worse bite than that of a shark had never looked into the jaws of a mermaid.

Actually, people knew very little about them. It was a fact that mermaids avoided humans. For many of the city's inhabitants, that was reason enough to hunt them. Young men often made a sport of driving inexperienced mermaids who'd gotten mixed up in the labyrinth of the Venetian canals into a corner; if one of them happened to die as a result, people thought that was too bad, certainly, but no one ever reproved the hunters.

But mostly the mermaids were caught and imprisoned in tanks in the Arsenal until a reason for keeping them was found. Often it was this boat race, more rarely fish soup—though the taste of their long, scaled tails was legendary, surpassing even delicacies like sea cows and whales.

"I feel sorry for them," said the second girl, sitting next to Merle in the gondola. She was just as under-nourished and even bonier. Her pale, almost white blond hair hung way down her back. Merle knew nothing about her companion, only that she also came from an orphanage, though from another district of Venice. She was a year younger than Merle, thirteen, she'd said. Her name was Junipa.

Junipa was blind.

"You feel sorry for the mermaids?" Merle asked.

The blind girl nodded. "I could hear their voices a while ago."

"But they haven't said anything."

"Yes, under the water," Junipa countered. "They were singing the whole time. I have quite good ears, you know. Many blind people do."

Merle stared at Junipa in astonishment, until she finally became conscious of how impolite that was, whether the girl could see it or not.

"Yes," said Merle, "me too. I feel they always seem a little . . . I don't know, melancholy somehow. As if they'd lost something that meant a lot to them."

"Their freedom?" suggested the gondolier, who had been listening to them.

"More than that," Merle replied. She couldn't find

the words to describe what she meant. "Maybe being able to be happy." That still wasn't exactly it, but it came close.

She was convinced that the mermaids were just as human as she was. They were more intelligent than many a person she'd learned to know in the orphanage, and they had feelings. They were *different,* certainly, but that didn't give anyone the right to treat them like animals, to harness them to their boats or chase them through the lagoon whenever they pleased. The Venetians' behavior toward them was cruel and utterly inhuman—all the things, really, that people said about the mermaids.

Merle sighed and looked down into the water. The prow of the gondola was cutting through the emerald green surface like a knife blade. In the narrow side canals the water was very calm; it was only on the Grand Canal that stronger waves came up sometimes. But here, three or four corners removed from Venice's main artery, there was complete stillness.

Soundlessly the gondola glided underneath arching bridges. Some were carved with grinning stone imps; bushy weeds were growing on their heads like tufts of green hair.

On both sides of the canal the fronts of the houses came straight down into the water. None was lower than four stories. A few hundred years before, when

Venice had still been a mighty trading power, goods had been unloaded from the canal directly into the palazzos of the rich merchant families. But today many of the old buildings stood empty, most of the windows were dark, and the wooden doors at the water level were rotten and eroded by dampness—and that not just since the Egyptian army's siege had closed around the city. The born-again pharaoh and his sphinx commanders were not to blame for all of it.

"Lions!" Junipa exclaimed suddenly.

Merle looked along the canal to the next bridge. She couldn't discover a living soul, to say nothing of the stone lions of the City Guard. "Where? I don't see any."

"I can smell them," Junipa insisted. She was sniffing at the air soundlessly, and out of the corner of her eye Merle saw the gondolier behind them shake his head in bewilderment.

She tried to emulate Junipa, but the gondola must have gone on for almost another two hundred feet before Merle's nostrils detected something: the odor of damp stone, musty and a little mildewed, so strong that it even masked the breath of the sinking city.

"You're right." It was unmistakably the stench of the stone lions used by the Venetian City Guard as riding animals and comrades-at-arms.

At that very moment one of the powerful animals appeared on a bridge ahead of them. It was of granite, one of the most common breeds among the stone lions of the lagoon. There were other, stronger ones, but that made no difference in the long run. Anyone who fell into the clutches of a granite lion was as good as lost. The lions had been the emblems of the city from time immemorial, back to the days when every one of them was winged and had been able to lift itself into the air. But today there were only a few who could do that, a strictly regulated number of single animals, which were reserved for the personal protection of the city councillors. The breeding masters on the island of the lions, up in the north of the lagoon, had bred out flying in all the others. They came into the world with stunted wings, which they bore as mournful appendages on their backs. The soldiers of the City Guard fastened their saddles to them.

The granite lion on the bridge also was only an ordinary animal of stone. Its rider wore the uniform of the Guard. A rifle dangled on a leather strap over his shoulder, pointedly casual, a sign of military arrogance. The soldiers had not been able to protect the city from the Egyptian Empire—instead, the Flowing Queen had done that—but since the proclamation of siege conditions thirty years before, the Guard had gained more and more power. Meanwhile they were surpassed in their arrogance only by their commanders, the city councillors, who managed affairs in the captive city as they saw fit. Perhaps the councillors and their soldiers were only trying to prove something to themselves—after all, everyone else knew that they weren't in a position to defend Venice in an emergency. But so long as the Flowing Queen kept the enemy far from the lagoon, they could rejoice in their omnipotence.

The guardsman on the bridge looked down into the gondola with a grin, then waved to Merle and gave the lion his spurs. With a snort the beast leaped forward. Merle could hear all too clearly the scraping of its stone claws on the pavement. Junipa held her ears. The bridge quivered and trembled under the paws of the great cat, and the sound seemed to careen back and forth between the high facades like a bouncing ball. Even the still water was set in motion. The gondola rocked gently.

The gondolier waited until the soldier had disappeared into the tangle of narrow streets, then spat into the water and murmured, "The Ancient Traitor take you!" Merle looked around at him, but the man looked past her down the canal, his face expressionless. Slowly he guided the gondola forward.

"Do you know how far it is now?" Junipa inquired of Merle.

Before she could answer, the gondolier replied, "We're there now. There ahead, just around the corner." Then he realized that "there ahead" was not information the blind girl could use. So he quickly added, "Only a few minutes, then we'll be on the Canal of the Expelled."

Narrowness and darkness—those were the two qualities that impressed themselves on Merle most strongly.

The Canal of the Expelled was flanked by tall houses, one as dark as the next. Almost all were abandoned. The window openings gaped empty and black in the gray fronts, many panes were broken, and the wooden shutters hung aslant on their hinges like wings on the ribs of dead birds. From one broken door came the snarling of fighting tomcats, nothing unusual in a city of umpteen thousand stray cats. Pigeons cooed on the window ledges, and the narrow, railingless walks on both sides of the water were covered with moss and pigeon droppings.

The only two inhabited houses stood out clearly from the rows of decaying buildings. They were exactly opposite one another and glared across the canal like two chess players, with furrowed faces and knitted brows. About three hundred feet separated them from the mouth of the canal and from its shadowy dead end. Each of the houses had a balcony, that of the one on the left of stone, that of the one on the right wrought of intertwining metal grill-work. The balustrades high over the water were almost touching.

The canal measured about three paces wide. The water, though still a brilliant green, looked darker and deeper here. The spaces between the old houses were so narrow that hardly any daylight reached the water's surface. A few bird feathers rocked languidly on the waves caused by the gondola.

Merle had a vague notion of what lay ahead of her. They had explained it to her at the orphanage, repeatedly mentioning how grateful she should feel that she was being sent here to apprentice. She would be spending the next few years on this canal, in this tunnel of greenish gray twilight.

The gondola neared the inhabited houses. Merle listened intently, but she could hear nothing except a distant murmur of indistinguishable voices. When she looked over at Junipa, she saw that every muscle in the blind girl's body was tensed; she had closed her eyes; her lips formed silent words—perhaps those she was picking out of the whisperings with her trained ears, like the movements of a carpet weaver, who with his sharp needle purposefully picks out a single thread from among thousands of others. Junipa was indeed an extraordinary girl.

The building on the left housed the weaving establishment of the famed Umberto. It was said to be wicked to wear garments that he and his apprentices made; his reputation was too bad, his quarrel with the Church too well known. But those women who allowed themselves to secretly order bodices and dresses from him swore behind their hands as to their magical effect. "Umberto's clothes make one slender," they said in the salons and streets of Venice. *Really* slender. For whoever wore them not only looked slimmer—she was in fact so, as if the magical threads of the master weaver drew off the fat of all those who were enveloped by them. The priests in Venice's churches had more than once thundered against the unholy dealings of the master weaver, so loudly and hatefully that the trade guild had finally expelled Umberto from its ranks.

But Umberto wasn't the only one who had come to feel the wrath of the guilds. It was the same with the master of the house opposite. There was also a workshop housed in that one, and it too devoted itself in its way to the service of beauty. However, no clothing was woven there, and its master, the honorable Arcimboldo, would doubtless have protested loudly at any open suggestion of a connection between him and his archenemy, Umberto.

ARCIMBOLDO'S GLASS FOR THE GODS was written in golden letters over the door, and right beside it was a sign: MAGIC MIRRORS FOR GOOD AND WICKED STEPMOTHERS, FOR BEAUTIFUL AND UGLY WITCHES, AND EVERY SORT OF HONEST PURPOSE.

"We're there," Merle said to Junipa, as her eye traveled over the words a second time. "Arcimboldo's magic mirror workshop."

"How does it look?" Junipa asked.

Merle hesitated. It wasn't easy to describe her first impression. The house was dark, certainly, like the whole canal and its surroundings, but next to the door stood a tub of colorful flowers, a friendly spot in the gray twilight. Only at the second look did she realize that the flowers were made of glass.

"Better than the orphanage," she said somewhat uncertainly.

The steps leading up to the walk from the water surface were slippery. The gondolier helped them both climb out. He had already been paid when he picked the girls up. He wished them both luck before he slowly glided away in his gondola.

They stood there a little lost, each with a half-full bundle in her hand, just under the sign offering magic mirrors for wicked stepmothers. Merle wasn't sure whether she should consider this a good or a bad introduction to her apprenticeship. Probably the truth lay somewhere in between.

Behind a window of the weaver's workshop on the other bank, a face whisked past, then a second. Curious apprentices, Merle guessed, who were looking over the new arrivals. *Enemy* apprentices, if you believed the rumors.

Arcimboldo and Umberto had never liked each other, that was no secret, and even their simultaneous expulsion from the trade guilds had changed nothing. Each one blamed the other. "What? Throw me out and not that crazy mirror maker?" Umberto was said to have asked loudly. The weaver asserted, on the other hand, that

Arcimboldo had cried at his own expulsion, "I'll go, but you'd do well to bring charges against that thread picker, too." Which of these accusations matched the truth, no one knew with utter certainty. It was clear only that they had both been expelled from the guilds because of forbidden trafficking with magic.

A magician, Merle thought excitedly, though she had been thinking of scarcely anything else for days. *Arcimboldo is a real magician!*

With a grating sound, the door of the mirror workshop was opened, and an odd-looking woman appeared on the pavement. Her long hair was piled up into a knot. She wore leather trousers, which emphasized her slender legs. Over these fluttered a white blouse, shot through with silver threads—Merle might have expected such a fine item in the weaver's workshop on the opposite bank of the canal, but not in the house of Arcimboldo.

But the most unusual thing was the mask behind which the woman hid a part of her face. The last Carnival of Venice—at one time famous the world over—had taken place over four decades ago. That had been 1854, three years after the Pharaoh Amenophis had been awakened to a new life in the stepped pyramid of Amun-Ka-Re. Today, in time of war, distress, and siege, there was no occasion to dress up.

And yet the woman was wearing a mask, formed of paper, enameled, and artfully decorated, doubtless the work of a Venetian artist. It covered the lower half of her face right up to her nostrils. Its surface was snow white and shone like porcelain. The mask maker had painted a small, finely curved mouth with dark red lips on it.

"Eft," the woman said, and then, with a barely noticeable lisp, "that's my name."

"Merle. And this is Junipa. We're the new apprentices."

"Of course, who else?" Only Eft's eyes betrayed that she was smiling. Merle wondered whether the woman's face could have been disfigured by illness.

Eft ushered the girls in. Beyond the door was a broad entrance hall, as in most of the houses of the city. It was only sparely furnished, the walls plastered and without hangings—precautions against the high waters that struck Venice some winters. The domestic life of the Venetians took place on the second and third floors, the ground floors being left bare and uncomfortable.

"It's late," said Eft, as if her eye had happened to fall on a clock. But Merle couldn't discover one anywhere. "Arcimboldo and the older students are in the workshop at this hour and may not be disturbed. You'll get to meet them in the morning. I'll show you to your room."

Merle couldn't repress a smile. She had hoped that she and Junipa would share a room. She saw that the blind girl was also happy to hear Eft's words.

The masked woman led them up the steps of a curving flight of stairs. "I'm the housekeeper for the workshop.

I'll be cooking for you and washing your things. Perhaps in the first few months you'll be giving me a hand with it; the master often requests that of newcomers—especially as you are the only girls in the house."

The only girls? That all the other apprentices could be boys hadn't occurred to Merle at all until now. She was all the more relieved that she was beginning her apprenticeship with Junipa.

The blind girl wasn't very talkative, and Merle guessed that she hadn't had a very easy time of it in the orphanage. Merle had only too often experienced how awful children can be, especially to those they consider weaker. Certainly Junipa's blindness would frequently have been a reason for mean tricks.

The girls followed Eft down a long hallway. The walls were hung with countless mirrors. Most were aimed toward each other: mirrors in mirrors in mirrors. Merle doubted that any of these were Arcimboldo's famous magic mirrors, for she could discover nothing unusual about them.

After Eft had explained all the rules about eating times, going out, and behavior in the house, Merle asked, "Who buys Arcimboldo's magic mirrors, anyhow?"

"You're curious," stated Eft, leaving it open as to whether this displeased her.

"Rich people?" Junipa queried, absently running her hand over her smooth hair.

"Perhaps," Eft replied. "Who knows?" With that she let the subject drop, and the girls probed no further. They would have time enough to find out everything important about the workshop and its customers. *Good and wicked stepmothers,* Merle repeated to herself. Beautiful and ugly witches. That sounded exciting.

The room that Eft showed them to was not large. It smelled musty, but since it was on the fourth floor of the building, it was pleasingly bright. In Venice you saw daylight only above the third floor, to say nothing of the sunshine, if you were lucky. However, the window of this room looked out over a sea of orange tiles. At night they would be able to see the starry heavens, and all day they would be able to see the sun—provided their work left them time for it.

The room was at the back of the house. Far below the window, Merle could make out a small courtyard with a round well in the center. All the houses opposite appeared to be empty. At the beginning of the war with the Pharaoh's kingdom, many Venetians had left the city and fled to the mainland—a disastrous mistake, as it later turned out.

Eft left the girls, telling them she would bring them something to eat in an hour. And then after that they should go to bed, so that they would be rested for their first workday.

Junipa felt along the bedposts and gently let herself

down on the mattress. Carefully she stroked the bedcover with both hands.

"Look at the blankets! So fluffy!"

Merle sat down beside her. "They must have been expensive," she said dreamily. In the orphanage the blankets had been thin and scratchy, and there were all kinds of bugs that bit your skin while you were asleep.

"It looks as though we've been lucky," Junipa said.

"We still haven't met Arcimboldo."

Junipa raised an eyebrow. "Anyone who takes a blind girl from an orphanage to teach her something can't be a bad man."

Merle remained skeptical. "Arcimboldo is known for that—taking orphans as pupils. Anyway, what parents would send their child to apprentice in a place that calls itself the Canal of the Expelled?"

"But I can't see, Merle! I've been nothing but a millstone around people's necks all my life."

"Did they make you think that at the home?" Merle gave Junipa a searching look. Then she took her narrow white hand. "Anyhow, I'm glad you're here."

Junipa smiled in embarrassment. "My parents abandoned me when I was just a year old. They left a note in my clothes. They said that they didn't want to raise a cripple."

"That's horrible."

"How did you land in the home?"

Merle sighed. "An attendant in the orphanage once

told me that they found me in a wicker basket floating on the Grand Canal." She shrugged her shoulders. "Sounds like a fairy tale, huh?"

"A sad one."

"I was only a few days old."

"Who would throw a child into the canal?"

"And who would abandon one because it couldn't see?"

They smiled at each other. Even though Junipa's blank eyes looked right through her, Merle still had the feeling that her glances were more than an empty gesture. Through hearing and touching Junipa probably perceived more than most other people.

"Your parents didn't want you to drown," Junipa declared. "Otherwise they wouldn't have taken the trouble to lay you in a wicker basket."

Merle looked at the floor. "They put something else in the basket. Would you like to—" She stopped.

"—see it?" Grinning, Junipa finished the sentence.

"I'm sorry."

"You don't have to be. I can still touch it. Do you have it with you?"

"Always, no matter where I go. Once, in the orphanage, a girl tried to steal it. I pulled all her hair out almost." She laughed a little shamefacedly. "Oh, well, I was only eight then."

Junipa laughed too. "Then I'd better put mine up in a knot for the night."

Merle touched Junipa's hair gently. It was thick and as light as a snow queen's.

"Well, so?" Junipa asked. "What else was in your wicker basket?"

Merle stood up, opened her bundle, and pulled out her most prized possession—to be precise, it was her only one, besides her sweater and the simple patched dress she had for a change of clothes.

It was a hand mirror, about as large as her face, oval and with a short handle. The frame was made of a dark metal alloy, which so many in the orphanage had greedily eyed as tarnished gold. In truth, however, it was not gold and also not any other metal anyone had ever heard of, for it was as hard as diamond.

But the most unusual thing about this mirror was its reflective surface. It wasn't made of glass, but of water. You could reach into it and make little waves, yet never a drop fell out, even when you turned the mirror.

Merle placed the handle in Junipa's open hand and carefully closed the blind girl's fingers around it. Instead of feeling the object, she first put it to her ear.

"It's whispering," she said softly.

Merle was surprised. "Whispering? I've never heard anything."

"You aren't blind, either." A small, vertical furrow had appeared in Junipa's forehead. She was concentrating. "There are several voices. I can't understand the words, there are too many voices, and they're too far away. But they're whispering with each other." Junipa lowered the mirror and ran the fingers of her left hand around the oval frame. "Is it a picture?" she asked.

"A mirror," Merle replied. "But—don't be scared—it's made of water."

Junipa betrayed no sign of astonishment, as if this were something entirely ordinary. Only, when she stretched out a fingertip and touched the water surface, she flinched. "It's cold," she said.

Merle shook her head. "No, not at all. The water in the mirror is always warm. And you can put something in it, but when you pull it out again, it's dry."

Junipa touched the water once more. "To me it feels ice-cold."

Merle took the mirror out of her hand and stuck her index and middle fingers in. "Warm," she said again, now almost a little defiantly. "It's never been cold, as long as I can remember."

"Has anyone else ever touched it? I mean, except you."

"Nobody so far. Just once, I gave permission to a nun who came to visit us in the orphanage, but she was terribly afraid of it and said it was a work of the Devil."

Junipa pondered. "Maybe the water feels cold to anyone else except the owner."

Merle frowned. "That could be." She looked at the

surface, which was always slightly in motion. Distorted and quivering, her reflection looked back.

"Are you planning to show it to Arcimboldo?" Junipa asked. "After all, he knows all about magic mirrors."

"I don't think so. At least not right away. Maybe later sometime."

"You're afraid he might take it away from you."

"Wouldn't you be?" Merle sighed. "It's the only thing that I have left of my parents."

"*You* are a part of your parents, don't forget."

Merle was quiet for a moment. She considered whether she could trust Junipa, whether she should tell the blind girl the whole truth. Finally, after a cautious glance toward the door, she whispered, "The water isn't everything."

"What do you mean?"

"I can stick my whole arm into the mirror and it doesn't come out on the other side." In fact, the back side of the oval was of the same hard metal as the frame.

"Will you do it now?" asked Junipa in astonishment. "I mean, right now this minute?"

"If you want." First Merle let her fingers slide into the interior of the water mirror, then her hand, finally her entire arm. It was as if it had vanished completely from this world.

Junipa reached out her hand and felt from Merle's shoulder to the rim of the mirror. "How does it feel?"

"Very warm," Merle reported. "Comfortable, but not

hot." She lowered her voice. "And sometimes I feel something else."

"What?"

"A hand."

"A . . . hand?"

"Yes. It grasps mine, very gently, and holds it."

"It holds you fast?"

"Not *fast*. Just . . . oh, well, it just holds my hand. The way friends do. Or—"

"Or parents?" Junipa was looking at her intently. "Do you believe that your father or your mother is in there holding your hand?"

It was uncomfortable for Merle to speak about it. Nevertheless, she felt that she could trust Junipa. After a brief hesitation, she overcame her shyness. "It could be possible, couldn't it? After all, they were the ones who put the mirror in the basket with me. Maybe they did it to stay in contact with me, so that I'd know that they are still . . . somewhere."

Junipa nodded slowly, but she didn't appear to be completely convinced. Rather, understanding. A little sadly she said, "For a long time I imagined that my father was a gondolier. I know that the gondoliers are the handsomest men in Venice. I mean, everyone knows that . . . even if I can't see them."

"They aren't *all* handsome," Merle objected.

Junipa's voice sounded dreamy. "And I imagined for

myself that my mother was a water carrier from the mainland."

People said that the water carrier women who sold drinking water on the streets from huge pitchers were the most attractive women far and wide. And as in the case of the gondoliers, this story did possess a kernel of truth.

Junipa went on, "So I used to imagine that my parents were both these two very beautiful people, as if that would say something about me. About my true self. I even tried to excuse them. Two such perfect creatures, I said to myself, couldn't see themselves with a sick child. I talked myself into thinking it was their right to abandon me." Suddenly she shook her head so hard that her pale blond hair flew wildly around her. "Today I know that's all non-sense. Perhaps my parents are good looking or perhaps they're ugly. Perhaps they aren't even alive anymore. But that has nothing to do with me, you understand? I'm me, that's the only thing that counts. And my parents did wrong because they simply threw a helpless child out onto the streets."

Merle had listened, perplexed. She knew what Junipa meant, even if she didn't understand what that had to do with her and the hand in her mirror.

"You mustn't fool yourself, Merle," said the blind girl, and she sounded much wiser than her years. "Your parents didn't want you. Therefore they put you in that wicker basket. And so if someone is reaching out a hand to you in your mirror, it doesn't necessarily have to be your father or your mother. That thing you are feeling is magic, Merle. And with magic you have to be careful."

For a moment Merle felt anger rising in her. Wounded, she told herself that Junipa had no right to say such a thing, to rob her of her hopes, all the dreams she had when the other person in the mirror held her hand. But then she understood that Junipa was only being honest and that honesty is the most beautiful gift that a person can give to another at the beginning of a friendship.

Merle shoved the mirror under her pillow. She knew that it wouldn't break and that she could press the pillow as hard as she wanted onto the surface of the water without it becoming wet or sucking up the liquid. Then she sat back down next to Junipa and put her arm around her. The blind girl returned the hug and so they held each other like sisters, like two people who have no secrets from each other. It was such an overpowering feeling of closeness and mutual understanding that for a while it even surpassed the warmth of the hand in the mirror and its calm and strength, with which it had won Merle's trust.

When the girls released each other, Merle said, "You can try it sometime, if you want."

"The mirror?" Junipa shook her head. "It's yours. If it wanted me to put my hand in, the water would have been warm for me."

Merle felt that Junipa was right. Whether it was the

hand of one of her parents that touched hers inside there or the fingers of something entirely different, it was clear that they accepted only Merle. It might even be dangerous if another person pushed so deeply into the space behind the mirror.

The girls were sitting there together on the bed when the door opened and Eft came in. She was bearing the evening meal on a wooden tray, substantial soup with vegetables and basil, along with some white bread and a pitcher of water from the well in the courtyard.

"Go to sleep when you've unpacked," lisped the woman behind the mask as she left the room. "You'll have all the time in the world to talk with each other."

Had Eft been eavesdropping? Did she know of the mirror under Merle's pillow? But, Merle told herself, she had no reason to mistrust the housekeeper. Eft had so far been very friendly and welcoming. The mere fact that she hid the lower part of her face behind a mask didn't make her an evil person.

She was thinking again about Eft's mask as she began to fall asleep, and half-asleep she wondered whether everyone didn't wear a mask sometimes.

A mask of joy, a mask of sorrow, a mask of indifference.

A mask of you-can't-see-me.

2

MIRROR EYES

IN A DREAM MERLE MET THE FLOWING QUEEN.

It seemed as if she were riding through the waters of the lagoon on a being of soft glass. Green and blue phantoms beat against them, millions of drops, as warm as the water inside her mirror. They caressed her cheeks, her neck, the palms of her open hands as she held them against the current. She felt that she was one with the Flowing Queen, a creature as unfathomable as the sunrise, as the power of thunder and lightning and the storm, as incomprehensible as life and death. They dove down under the surface, but Merle had no trouble breathing, for the

Queen was in her and kept her alive, as if they were two parts of one body.

Swarms of shimmering fish traveled along beside them, accompanying them on their journey, whose destination became less and less important to Merle. It was the journey alone that mattered, the oneness with the Flowing Queen, the feeling of comprehending the lagoon and sharing in its beauty.

And although nothing else happened, other than her gliding along with the Flowing Queen, it was a dream more marvelous than any Merle had dreamed for months, for years. In the orphanage her nights had consisted of cold, the bite of the fleas, and the fear of theft. But here, in the house of Arcimboldo, she was finally safe.

Merle awoke. In the first moment she thought that a sound had snatched her from sleep. But there was nothing. Complete silence.

The Flowing Queen. Everyone had heard of her. And yet no one knew what she really was. When the galleys of the Egyptians had tried to enter the Venetian lagoon, after their campaigns of extermination all over the world, something unusual had happened. Something wonderful. The Flowing Queen had put them to flight. The Egyptian Empire, the greatest and most horrific power in the history of the world, had had to withdraw with its tail between its legs.

Since then, the legends had twined about the Flowing Queen.

It was certain she was not a creature of flesh and blood. She was in and throughout the waters of the lagoon, the narrow canals of the city, as well as the broad expanses of water between the islands. The city councillors maintained that they had regular conversations with her and acted according to her wishes. If in fact she had ever begun to speak, however, it was never in the presence of the simple folk.

Some said she was only as big as a droplet that was sometimes here, sometimes there; others swore she was the water itself, some just a tiny swallow. She was more power than creature, and for many even a deity, who was in every thing and every creature.

The campaigns of the tyrants might sow grief, death, and desolation, Amenophis and his Empire might subjugate the world—but the aura of the Flowing Queen had protected the lagoon for more than thirty years now, and so there was no one in the city who did not feel obligated to her. In the churches Masses were held in her honor, the fishermen sacrificed a portion of every catch, and even the secret guild of the thieves showed her gratitude by keeping their hands to themselves on certain days in the year.

There—again a sound! This time there was no doubt about it.

Merle sat up in bed. The tendrils of her dreams still

lapped at her senses like the foaming tide at one's feet during a walk on the beach.

The sound was repeated. Metal grating on metal, coming up from the courtyard. Merle recognized that sound—the lid of the well. It sounded the same way all over Venice when the heavy metal covers over the wells were opened. The cisterns existed all over the city, in every open piazza and in most courtyards. Their round walls were carved with patterns and fabulous creatures of stone. Gigantic semicircular covers protected the precious drinking water from dirt and rats.

But who was busying himself about a well at this time of night? Merle got up and wiped the sleep from her eyes. A little wobbly on her legs, she went over to the window.

She was just in time to see in the moonlight a form climb over the edge of the well and slide into the dark well shaft. A moment later hands reached out of the darkness, grasped the edge of the lid, and pulled it, grating, over the opening.

Merle emitted a sharp gasp. Instinctively she ducked, although the form had disappeared into the well long since.

Eft! There was no doubt that she had been the shadowy figure in the courtyard. But what would make the housekeeper climb into a well in the middle of the night?

Merle turned around, intending to wake Junipa.

The bed was empty.

"Junipa?" she whispered tensely. But there was no corner of the small room she could not have seen from there. No hiding place.

Unless . . .

Merle bent and looked under both beds. But there was no trace of the girl.

She went to the door. It had no bolt that the girls could have slid closed for the night, no lock. Outside in the hallway it was utterly quiet.

Merle took a deep breath. The floor under her naked feet was bitterly cold. Quickly she pulled her dress and sweater on over her nightgown and pushed her feet into her worn-out leather shoes; they reached beyond her ankle and had to be tied, which at the moment required much too much time. But she couldn't possibly go looking for Junipa and run the danger of tripping over her own shoelaces. Hastily she laced and tied them, but her fingers trembled, and it took twice as long as usual.

Finally she slipped out into the passageway and pulled the door closed behind her. An ominous hissing came from somewhere in the distance. It didn't sound like an animal, more like a steam engine, but she wasn't sure whether it was coming from here in the house. Soon after, she heard it again, followed by a rhythmic pounding. Then silence again. Only as she was already on her way down the stairs did it occur to Merle that there were only two inhabited houses on the Canal of the Expelled—

Arcimboldo's workshop and that of the weaver on the other side.

The whole house smelled strange, a little of lubricating oil, of polished steel, and the acrid odor she knew from the glass workshops on the lagoon island of Murano. She had been there one single time, when an old glassmaker had contemplated taking her to work for him. Right after she arrived, he ordered her to scrub his back in the bath. Merle had waited until he was sitting in the water and then run as fast as she could back to the landing point. Stowing away in a boat, she'd managed to get back to the city. Such cases were not unknown at the orphanage, and although the authorities weren't at all happy to see her again, they had enough decency not to send her back to Murano.

Merle reached the landing on the third floor. Until then she'd met no one and discovered no sign of life. Where might the other apprentices be sleeping? Perhaps on the fourth floor, like her and Junipa. She knew at least that Eft was not in the house, but she avoided giving too much thought to what the odd woman was looking for in the well.

There remained only Arcimboldo himself. And, of course, Junipa. What if she'd only had to go to the bathroom? The tiny chamber, in which a round shaft in the floor ran straight down to the canal, was on the fourth floor too. Merle hadn't thought to look there, and now she cursed herself for it. She'd forgotten the most obvious thing—perhaps because in the orphanage it was always a bad sign when one of the children disappeared from his or her bed at night. Only a few of them ever reappeared again.

She was about to turn around to look, when the hissing started again. It sounded even more artificial, machine-like, and the tone made her shudder.

She thought she heard something else, too, very briefly only, soft in the background of the hissing.

A sob.

Junipa!

Merle tried to make out something in the dark stairwell. The area was pitch-black, only a touch of moonlight falling through a high window beside her, a vague suggestion of light that scarcely sufficed to make out the steps under her feet. In the hallway to her left ticked a grandfather clock, alone in the shadows, a monstrous outline like a coffin that someone had leaned against the wall.

Meanwhile she was certain: The hissing and the sobbing were coming from the interior of the house. From farther below. From the workshop on the second floor.

Merle hastened down the steps. The corridor that branched off from the staircase had a high, arching ceiling. She followed it, as softly and quickly as she could. Her throat was tight. Her breathing sounded as loud to her as the wheezing of one of the steamboats on the Grand Canal. What if she and Junipa had jumped out of the frying pan into the fire? If Arcimboldo had planned some horror similar to that of the old glassblower on Murano?

She recoiled as she perceived a movement next to her. But it was only her own reflection, flitting across the innumerable mirrors on the walls.

The hissing was coming more often now, and sounded nearer. Eft hadn't shown them exactly where the entrance to the workshop was. She'd merely mentioned that it was on the second floor. But here there were several doors, and all were high and dark and closed. There was nothing for Merle to do but follow the sounds. The soft sobbing had not been repeated. The thought of Junipa being helplessly delivered to an unknown danger brought tears to Merle's eyes.

One thing was certain in any case: She would not let anything happen to her new friend, even if it meant both of them being sent back to the orphanage. Of the worst she didn't want to think at all. Nevertheless, the bad thoughts stole into her mind like the buzzing of small gnats:

It's nighttime. And dark. Many people have disappeared into the canals already. No one would care about two girls. Two fewer mouths to feed, nothing more.

The corridor made a bend to the right. At its end glowed the outline of arched double doors. The crack between the two doors shimmered golden like wire that has been held in a candle flame. A strong fire must be burning inside the workshop—the coal boiler of the machine that was uttering the primeval hissing and snorting.

When Merle approached the door on tiptoe, she saw that a layer of smoke lay over the stone flags of the corridor like a fine ground fog. The smoke was coming from under the door, emerging in a fiery shimmer.

What if a fire had broken out in the workshop? *You have to remain calm,* Merle kept drumming into herself. *Very, very calm.*

Her feet stirred the smoke on the floor, conjuring up the outlines of foggy ghosts in the darkness, many times enlarged and distorted as shadows on the walls. The only light was the glow of the crack around the doors.

Darkness, fog, and the glowing doors directly in front of her—it seemed to Merle like the entrance to Hell, so unreal, so oppressive.

The acrid odor that she'd noticed in the upper stairwell was even more penetrating here. The lubricating oil stench was also stronger. It was rumored that messengers from Hell had visited the City Council in the past months and offered it the help of their master in the battle against the Empire. But the councillors had ruled out any pact with Old Nick. So long as the Flowing Queen was protecting them all, there was no reason for it. Ever since the National Geographic Society expedition under the famed Professor Charles Burbridge in 1833 had proven Hell to be a real place in the interior of the earth, there had been several meetings between the ambassadors of Satan and representatives of humanity. However, no one knew any of the details, and that was probably just as well.

All this shot through Merle's head while she walked the last paces up to the door of the workshop. With infinite caution she placed her hand flat on the wood. She'd expected it to feel warm, but that proved to have been wrong. The wood was cool and in no way different from any of the other doors in the house. Even the metal door handle was cold when Merle ran a finger over it.

She considered whether she should enter. It was the only thing she could do. She was alone, and she doubted there was anyone in this house who would come to her aid.

She'd just made her decision when the latch was pressed from the other side. Merle whirled around, meaning to flee, but then she sprang into the protection of the left-hand door, while the right one swung to the inside.

A broad beam of glowing light splashed across the smoke on the floor. Where Merle had just been standing, the swirls of smoke were swept aside by a draft of air. Then a shadow crossed the light stripe. Someone walked out into the corridor.

Merle pressed herself as deeply as she could into the protection of the closed side of the door. She was less than six feet away from the figure.

Shadows can make people menacing, even if in reality

they aren't at all. They make midgets large and weaklings as broad as elephants. So it was in this case.

The mighty shadow shrank, the farther the little old man got from the source of the light. As he stood there, without even noticing Merle, he looked almost a bit comical in his much too long trousers and the smock that had become almost black with soot and smoke. He had disheveled gray hair that stood out on all sides. His face glistened. A droplet of sweat ran down his temple and was lost in his bushy side whiskers.

Instead of turning around to Merle, he turned back to the door and extended a hand in the direction of the light. A second shadow melted with his on the floor.

"Come, my child," he said, his voice gentle. "Come out."

Merle didn't move. She hadn't imagined her first meeting with Arcimboldo like this. Only the calm and serenity in the old man's voice gave her a little hope.

But then the mirror maker said, "The pain will stop soon."

Pain?

"You needn't be afraid," Arcimboldo said, facing the open door. "You'll quickly get used to it, believe me."

Merle scarcely dared breathe.

Arcimboldo took two or three steps backward into the passageway. As he moved, he held both hands outstretched, an invitation to follow him.

"Come closer . . . yes, just like that. Very slowly."

And Junipa came. With small, uncertain steps she walked through the door into the hallway. She moved stiffly and very carefully.

But she can't see anything, Merle thought desperately. Why was Arcimboldo letting her wander around without help in a place that wasn't familiar to her? Why didn't he wait until she could take his hand? Instead he kept moving backward, farther from the door—and in fact at any moment he was going to discover Merle, hiding in the shadow. Spellbound, she stared at Junipa, who was falteringly stepping past her in the hallway. Arcimboldo, too, only had eyes for the girl.

"You're doing very well," he said encouragingly. "Very, very well."

The smoke on the floor gradually dispersed. No new clouds came from the depths of the workshop. The glowing firelight bathed the hallway in flickering, dark orange.

"It's all so . . . blurry," Junipa whispered miserably.

Blurry? Merle thought in astonishment.

"That will improve soon," said the mirror maker. "Just wait—early tomorrow, by daylight, everything will look very different. You must only trust me. Come just a little closer."

Junipa's steps were more confident now. Her careful progress was not because she couldn't see. Quite the contrary.

"What do you recognize?" asked Arcimboldo. "What exactly?"

"I don't know. Something is moving."

"Those are only shadows. Don't be afraid."

Merle couldn't believe her ears. Was it possible, was it actually possible that Arcimboldo had given Junipa sight?

"I've never seen before," said Junipa, baffled. "I was always blind."

"Is the light that you see red?" the mirror maker wanted to know.

"I don't know how light looks," she replied uncertainly. "And I don't know any colors."

Arcimboldo grimaced, annoyed with himself. "Stupid of me. I should have thought of that." He stopped and waited until he could grasp Junipa's outstretched hands. "You'll have a lot to learn in the next weeks and months."

"But that's why I came here."

"Your life will change, now that you can see."

Merle could no longer stay in her hiding place. Unmindful of all consequences, she leaped from the shadows into the light.

"What have you done to her?"

Startled, Arcimboldo looked over at her. And Junipa blinked. She strained to make anything out. "Merle?" she asked.

"I'm here." Merle walked up to Junipa and touched her gently on the arm.

"Ah, our second new pupil." Arcimboldo had quickly recovered from his surprise. "A quite curious pupil, it seems to me. But that doesn't matter. You would have found out early tomorrow morning in any case. So you are Merle."

She nodded. "And you are Arcimboldo."

"Indeed, indeed."

Merle looked from the old mirror maker back to Junipa. The realization of what he'd done found her unprepared. At first glance and in the weak light the change hadn't caught her attention, but now she asked herself how she could have overlooked *that*. It felt as though an ice-cold hand were running its fingers up her back.

"But . . . how . . . ?"

Arcimboldo smiled proudly. "Remarkable, isn't it?"

Merle couldn't speak a syllable. Dumbly she stared at Junipa.

Into her face.

At her eyes.

Junipa's white eyeballs had vanished. Instead of them, silvery mirrors glittered under her lids, set into her eye sockets. Not rounded like eyeballs, but flat. Arcimboldo had replaced Junipa's eyes with the splinters of a crystal mirror.

"What have you—"

Arcimboldo gently interrupted her. "Done to her?

Nothing, my child. She can see, at least a little. But that will improve from day to day."

"She has mirrors in her eyes!"

"That is so."

"But . . . but that's . . ."

"Magic?" Arcimboldo shrugged his shoulders. "Some might call it so. I call it science. Besides humans and animals there is only one other thing in the world that is able to see. Look in a mirror, and it will look back at you. That is the first lesson in my workshop, Merle. Mark it well. Mirrors can see."

"He's right, Merle," Junipa agreed. "I actually can see something. And I have the feeling that with every minute it's getting to be a little more."

Arcimboldo nodded delightedly. "That's wonderful!" He grabbed Junipa's hand and did a little dance of joy with her, just carefully enough not to pull her off her feet. The last remnants of the smoke flew up around them. "Say it yourself, isn't it fantastic?"

Merle stared at the two of them and couldn't quite believe what was taking place before her eyes. Junipa, who'd been blind since she was born, could see. Thirteen years of darkness had ended. And for that she had to thank Arcimboldo, this little wisp of a man with the disheveled hair.

"Help your friend to your room," said the mirror maker, after he'd let go of Junipa. "You have a strenuous day ahead of you tomorrow. Every day is strenuous in my workshop. But I think it will please you. Oh, yes, I really think so."

He held out his hand to Merle and added, "Welcome to Arcimboldo's house."

A little dazed, she remembered what they'd hammered into her in the orphanage. "Many thanks for having us here," she said politely. But in her confusion she hardly heard what she was saying. She looked after the gleeful old man as he hastened back into his workshop with dancing steps and pulled the door closed behind him.

Merle shyly took Junipa's hand and helped her up the stairs to the fourth floor, anxiously asking every few steps whether the pain was really not too bad. Whenever Junipa turned toward her, Merle shivered a little. She wasn't seeing her friend in the mirror eyes but only herself, reflected twice and slightly distorted. She reassured herself with the thought that it was certainly only a matter of getting used to Junipa's appearance until it looked completely normal to her.

But still, a slight doubt remained. Before, Junipa's eyes had been milky and unseeing. Now they were as cold as polished steel.

"I can see, Merle. I can really see."

Junipa kept murmuring the words to herself long after they were back in their own beds again.

Once, hours later, Merle awakened from tangled

dreams when she again heard the grating of the well cover, deep in the courtyard and very, very far away.

The first few days in Arcimboldo's mirror workshop were tiring, for Merle and Junipa were left to do all those jobs that the three older apprentices, boys, didn't want to do. So, many times a day Merle had to sweep up the fine mirror crystals that were deposited on the workshop floor like the desert sand that in some summers was driven across the sea as far as Venice.

As Arcimboldo had promised, Junipa's vision improved from day to day. She still perceived hardly more than ghostly images, but she was already able to differentiate one from another, and it was important to her to find her way around the unfamiliar workshop without help. However, they gave her easier jobs than Merle's, even if not much pleasanter ones. She was allowed no real recuperation after the stresses of that first night, and she had to weigh out endless quantities of quartz sand from sacks and put it into measures. What exactly Arcimboldo did with it remained a puzzle to the girls for the time being.

Actually, the mirror workshop under Arcimboldo appeared to have little to do with that long-standing tradition of which people in Venice had been proud since time out of mind. Earlier, in the sixteenth century, only the select were initiated into the art of mirror making. They all lived under strict watch on the glassblowing island of

Murano. There they lived in luxury, lacking for nothing—except freedom. For as soon as they had begun their training, they might never again leave the island. And for those who tried anyway, it was death. The agents of La Serenissima hunted down renegade mirror makers throughout Europe and killed the traitors before they could pass on the secret of mirror production to outsiders. Murano's mirrors were the only ones to adorn all the great houses of the nobility of Europe, for only in Venice was this art understood. As for the city, the secret could not be weighed in gold—well, except in the individual instances. Finally some mirror makers did succeed in fleeing from Murano and selling their secret art to the French, who then repaid them by killing them. Soon afterward the French opened their own workshops and robbed Venice of its monopoly. Mirrors were soon produced in many lands, and the prohibitions and punishments for Murano's mirror makers receded into oblivion.

Arcimboldo's mirrors, however, had as much to do with alchemy as with the art of glass making. After only the first few days, Merle sensed that it might be years before he would initiate her into his secrets. It was the same with the three boys. The eldest, Dario, though he'd already lived in the house for more than two years, had not the slightest glimmer of how Arcimboldo's art worked. Certainly they observed, even eavesdropped and spied, but they did not know the true secret.

Slim, black-haired Dario was the leader of
Arcimboldo's apprentices. When the master was pres-
ent, he always displayed very good behavior, but on his
own he was still the same lout he'd been when he came
from the orphanage two years before. During their short
free periods he was a braggart, and sometimes domi-
neering, too, though the two other boys had to suffer
more from that than Merle and Junipa did. In fact, to a
large extent he preferred to ignore the girls. It displeased
him that Arcimboldo had taken girls on as apprentices,
probably also because his behavior toward Eft left much
to be desired. He seemed to be afraid that Merle and
Junipa would take the housekeeper's side in arguments
or might betray some of his little secrets to her—such
as the fact that he regularly sampled Arcimboldo's
good red wine, which Eft kept under lock and key in
the kitchen. She didn't know that Dario had labori-
ously made himself a copy of the key to the cupboard.
Merle had discovered Dario's thieving by accident on
the third night, when she'd met him with a pitcher of
wine in the dark in the passageway. It never occurred
to her to use this observation to her own advantage,
but obviously that was exactly what Dario feared.
From that moment he had treated her even more
coolly, with downright hostility, even if he didn't dare
start an overt quarrel with her. Most of the time he gave
her the cold shoulder—which, to be precise, was more

notice than he bestowed on Junipa. She seemed not to exist at all for him.

Secretly Merle asked herself just why Arcimboldo had taken the rebellious Dario into his house. But that also raised the uncomfortable question of what he had found in *her*, and to that no answer had occurred to her as yet. Junipa might be an ideal subject for his experiment with the mirror shards—the girls had learned that he'd never dared anything like that before—but what was it that had prompted him to rescue Merle from the orphanage? He'd never met her and must have relied entirely on what the attendants could report about her—and Merle doubted that Arcimboldo had heard too much good about her from them. In the home they had considered her uncooperative and cheeky—words that in the vocabulary of the attendants stood for intellectually curious and self-confident.

As for the other two apprentices, they were only a year older than Merle. One was a pale-skinned, red-haired boy, whose name was Tiziano. The other—smaller and with a slight harelip—was named Boro. The two seemed to enjoy finally not being the youngest any longer and being able to boss Merle around, although their behavior never deteriorated into meanness. When they saw that the delegated work was getting to be too much, they readily helped, without being asked to. Junipa, on the other hand, they seemed to find uncanny, and Boro, especially, preferred to give her a wide berth. The boys accepted Dario as their

leader. They didn't have the doglike devotion to him that
Merle had sometimes seen with gangs in the orphanage,
but they clearly looked up to him. Anyway, he'd been
apprenticed to Arcimboldo a year longer than the two of
them had.

After about a week and a half, shortly before midnight, Merle saw Eft climbing down into the well a second time. She briefly considered waking Junipa but then
decided against it. She stood motionless at the window
for a while, staring at the well cover, then uneasily lay
down in her bed again.

She'd already told Junipa of her discovery on one of
their first evenings in the house.

"And she really climbed into the well?" Junipa had
asked.

"I just told you so!"

"Maybe the rope had come off the water bucket."

"Would you climb down into a pitch-black well in the
middle of the night just because some rope was broken? If
it really had been that, she could have done it in the day-
time. Besides, then she would have sent one of us." Merle
shook her head decidedly. "She didn't even have a lamp
with her."

Junipa's mirror eyes reflected the moonlight that was
shining in through their window that night. It looked as
though they were glowing in the white, icy light. As so
often, Merle had to repress a shudder. Sometimes at such

moments she had the feeling that Junipa saw more with her new eyes than just the surface of people and things—almost as if she could look directly into Merle's innermost thoughts.

"Are you afraid of Eft?" Junipa asked.

Merle thought about it briefly. "No. But you must admit that she's strange."

"Perhaps we all would be, if we had to wear a mask."

"And why does she wear it, anyhow? No one except Arcimboldo seems to know. I even asked Dario."

"Maybe you should just ask her sometime."

"That wouldn't be polite, if it really is an illness."

"What else would it be?"

Merle said nothing. She'd been asking herself these questions. She had a suspicion, only a very vague one; since it had come into her mind, she couldn't get it out of her head. Nevertheless, she thought it was better not to tell Junipa about it.

Merle and Junipa hadn't spoken about Eft again since that evening. There were so many other things to talk about, so many new impressions, discoveries, challenges. Every day was a new adventure, especially for Junipa, whose vision was fast improving. Merle envied her a little for how easily she became enthusiastic about the smallest things; but at the same time she rejoiced with her over the unexpected cure.

The morning after Merle saw Eft climb down into the

well the second time, something happened that once again turned her thoughts from the housekeeper's secret activities: the first meeting with the apprentices on the other bank of the canal, the apprentices of Master Weaver Umberto.

Merle had almost forgotten about the weaving workshop during the eleven days that she'd been living in the mirror maker's house. There'd been no trace of the well-known quarrel between the two masters, which had once been the talk of all Venice. Merle hadn't left the house at all during this period. Her entire day was spent mainly in the workshop, the adjoining storerooms, the dining room, and her room. Now and again one of the apprentices had to accompany Eft when she went to the vegetable market on Rio San Barnaba, but so far the housekeeper's choice had always fallen on one of the boys; they were bigger and could carry the heavy crates without any difficulty.

So Merle was caught completely unprepared when the students from the other side brought the quarrel forcefully to mind. As she later learned, it had been a tradition for years among the apprentices of both houses to play tricks on each other, which not infrequently ended with broken glass, cursing masters, bruises, and abrasions. The last of these attacks had been three weeks before and was credited to Dario, Boro, and Tiziano. The weaver boys' retaliation was long overdue after that.

Merle didn't find out why they'd chosen this morning,

and she was also not sure how they'd succeeded in getting inside the house—although later it was suspected they'd laid a board across the canal from one balcony railing to the other and so had balanced their way to the mirror maker's side. That they did all this in broad daylight, and during working hours, was a sign that it had been done with Umberto's blessing, just as earlier trespasses by Dario and the others had taken place with Arcimboldo's agreement.

Merle was just about to begin gluing the wooden frame of a mirror when there was a clatter at the entrance to the workshop. Alarmed, she looked up. She was afraid Junipa had stumbled over a tool.

But it wasn't Junipa. A small figure had slipped on a screwdriver and was staggering, fighting for balance. Its face was hidden behind a bear mask of enameled paper. With one hand it flailed wildly in the air, while the bag of paint it had held in the other burst on the tiles in a blue star.

"*Weavers!*" Tiziano bellowed, dropping his work and jumping up.

"Weavers! Weavers!" Boro, in another corner of the workshop, took up his friend's cry, and soon Dario also thundered in.

Merle got up from her place in irritation. Her eyes traveled uncertainly around the room. She didn't understand what was going on, ignorant of the competition among the apprentices.

The masked boy at the entrance slipped on his own paint and crashed on the seat of his pants. Before Dario and the others could laugh at him or even go for him, three other boys appeared in the corridor, all wearing colorful paper masks. One in particular caught Merle's eye: It was the visage of a splendid fabulous beast, half man, half bird. The long, curving beak was lacquered golden, and tiny glass gems glittered in the painted eyebrows.

Merle didn't have a chance to look at the other masks, for already a whole squadron of paint bags was flying in her direction. One burst at her feet and sprayed sticky red, another hit her shoulder and bounced off without bursting. It rolled away, over to Junipa, who'd been standing there with a gigantic broom in her hand, not quite knowing what was happening all around her. But now she grasped the situation and quickly bent, grabbed the paint bag, and flung it back at the invaders. The boy with the bear mask sprang to one side, and the missile hit the bird face behind him. The bag burst on the point of the bill and covered its owner with green paint.

Dario cheered, and Tiziano thumped Junipa encouragingly on the shoulder. Then the second wave of attacks followed. This time they didn't get off so lightly. Boro, Tiziano, and Merle were hit and spotted over and over with paint. Out of the corner of her eye, Merle saw Arcimboldo, cursing, close the door of the mirror storeroom and bar it from inside. His students might break heads, so long as the finished mirrors remained unharmed.

The apprentices were left to their own devices. Four against four. Really even five against four, if you counted Junipa—after all, in spite of her weak eyes, she'd scored the first hit for the mirror makers.

"It's the student weavers from the other bank," Boro called to Merle as he grabbed a broom, wielding it like a sword with both hands. "No matter what happens, we have to defend the workshop."

Typical boy, thought Merle, as she patted a little help-lessly at the paint on her dress. But why did they con-stantly have to prove themselves with such nonsense?

She looked up—and was hit on the forehead with another paint bag. Viscous yellow poured over her face and her shoulders.

That did it! With an angry cry she grabbed up the glue bottle, whose contents she'd been using to glue the mirror frame, and hurled herself at the first available weaver boy. It was the one with the bear mask. He saw her coming and tried to grab another paint bag from his shoulder bag. Too late! Merle was already there. She hurled him over back-ward with a blow, fell on him with her knees on his chest, and shoved the narrow end of the glue bottle into the left eye opening.

"Close your eyes!" she warned and pumped a strong jet of glue under the mask. The boy swore, then his words were lost in a blubber, followed by a long drawn-out "Aaaaaaaahhhhhhh!"

She saw that her opponent was out of action for the moment, pushed herself off him, and leaped back up. She now was holding the glue bottle like a pistol, even if it didn't make much sense, for most of the contents had been sprayed out. Out of the corner of her eye she saw Boro and Tiziano scuffling with two weaver boys, a wild fight. The mask of one of the boys was already demolished. Instead of joining in, however, Merle ran over to Junipa, grabbed her by the arm, and pulled her behind one of the workbenches.

"Don't move from that spot," she whispered to her.

Junipa protested. "I'm not as helpless as you think."

"No, certainly not." Merle glanced at the boy with the bird mask. His upper body was green from Junipa's paint bag. "Nevertheless, better stay under cover. This can't last much longer."

As she sprang up, she saw that her triumph had been too early. Tiziano's opponent had gained the upper hand again. And there was no sign of Dario anywhere. Merle first discovered him when suddenly he was standing in the doorway. In his hand gleamed one of the knives Arcimboldo used to trim the whisper-thin silver sheets for the backs of the mirrors. The blade wasn't long, but it was razor sharp.

"Serafin!" called Dario to the boy with the bird mask. "Come on, if you dare."

The weaver's boy saw the knife in Dario's hand and took up the challenge. His three companions retreated to the entrance. Boro helped Tiziano to his feet and then pushed Merle to the edge of the workshop.

"Have they gone crazy?" she gasped breathlessly. "They're going to kill each other."

Boro's frown betrayed that he shared her concern. "Dario and Serafin have hated each other since they first laid eyes on each other. Serafin's the leader of the weavers. He cooked up this whole thing."

"That's no reason to go at him with a knife."

While they were speaking, Dario and Serafin had met in the center of the room. Merle noticed that Serafin moved with light feet, like a dancer. He skillfully avoided the clumsy attacks of Dario, whose knife cut silvery traces in the air. Before Dario realized it, the weaver boy had extracted the knife from his fingers. With a cry of fury, Dario rushed at his opponent and landed a treacherous punch on his Adam's apple. The yellow bird face flew to one side and revealed Serafin's face. His cheekbones were finely cut, a few freckles sprinkled the bridge of his nose. He had blond hair, not so light as Junipa's; the green paint had clumped it into strings.

The weaver's bright blue eyes were squinting angrily. Before Dario could avoid it, Serafin landed a punch that flung the student mirror maker against the workbench behind which Junipa had taken shelter. Dario made one leap over the bench to put it between himself and his opponent. Junipa moved back a step in fear. But Serafin followed Dario around the bench and was about to grab him again. Dario's nose was bleeding; the last blow had weakened him. Instead of facing his antagonist, he whirled around, grabbed the surprised Junipa by the shoulders with both hands, pulled her roughly in front of him, and gave her a powerful push, which sent her stumbling in Serafin's direction.

Merle uttered a scream of rage. "That coward!"

The weaver boy saw Junipa flying toward him and saw Dario as well, just behind her, ready to use his chance. Serafin had a choice: He could catch Junipa to keep her from plunging into a rack of glass bottles—or he could sidestep her and attack his archfoe.

Serafin made a quick grab. He caught Junipa and held her for a moment in an embrace that was intended to protect her as well as to reassure her. "It's all right," he whispered to her, "nothing happened to you."

He'd scarcely spoken the words when Dario rammed his fist over Junipa's shoulder into Serafin's face.

"No!" bellowed Merle furiously. She leaped past Boro and Tiziano, ran to the workbench, and pulled Dario away from Junipa and Serafin.

"What are you doing?" yelped the older boy, but she'd already pulled him over backward to the floor.

Very briefly she caught Serafin's look as he carefully

pushed Junipa to one side. He smiled through green paint and blood, then hurried back to his friends at the entrance.

"We're clearing out," he said, and a moment later the weavers were gone.

Merle paid no attention to Dario but turned to Junipa, who was standing, dazed, in front of the bottle rack.

"Everything all right?"

Junipa nodded. "Yes . . . thanks. All right."

Behind Merle's back Dario began to curse and scold; she could sense that he was approaching her threateningly. She abruptly whirled around, looked deep into his small eyes, and gave him a box on the ear as hard as she could.

Before Dario could rush at her, Eft was suddenly between them. Merle felt the powerful grip when the housekeeper grasped her by the shoulder and pulled her away from Dario. But she didn't hear what Eft said, didn't hear the crude raging of Dario, which couldn't touch her. She was looking pensively out into the corridor into which Serafin had vanished with his friends.

3

EFT'S STORY

"And what, pray, am I supposed to do with you now?"

The master's voice sounded more disappointed than angry. Arcimboldo was sitting behind his study desk in the library. The walls of the room were covered with leather book spines. Merle wondered whether he'd actually read all those books.

"The damage the weaver's apprentices have caused with their paint is hardly worth mentioning, in light of what the two of you have done," Arcimboldo continued, letting his eyes travel from Dario to Merle and back again. The two were standing in front of the desk and looking sheepishly at the floor. Their anger at each other was in no way cooled, but even Dario seemed to understand that it was appropriate to restrain himself.

"You have kindled strife among the students. And you have led others to take sides. If Eft hadn't intervened, Junipa, Boro, and Tiziano would have had to choose for one of you." An angry spark appeared in the old man's eyes, so that he now seemed stern and unapproachable. "I cannot allow my apprentices to be divided. What I insist on is cooperation and avoidance of all unnecessary conflicts. Magic mirrors require a certain harmony in order to mature into what they are. In an atmosphere of hostility a shadow is laid over the glass that will make it grow blind."

Merle had the feeling that he was making it up. He wanted to talk them into feeling guilty. It would have suited that purpose better if he hadn't referred so plainly to "unnecessary conflicts": After all, it had been the childish quarrel between him and Umberto in the first place that caused this whole upset.

Sooner or later it would have come to a break between her and Dario anyhow, she'd felt that on the very first day. She surmised that Arcimboldo had foreseen it too. Did he regret taking her from the orphanage? Would she have to go back to the dirt and the poverty now?

Despite her fears, no feelings of guilt troubled her. Dario was a whining coward, as he'd just demonstrated twice: once when he went for Serafin with the knife, and the second time when he'd taken cover behind the defenseless Junipa. He'd richly deserved his box on the ear and, if it had been up to her, a good beating right afterward.

Clearly Arcimboldo saw it very similarly. "Dario," he said, "for your unworthy and unrestrained behavior you will clean the workshop by yourself. I don't want to find one single spot of paint tomorrow morning early. Understand?"

"And what about her?" Dario growled, pointing angrily at Merle.

"Did you understand me?" Arcimboldo asked once more, his bushy eyebrows drawing together like two thunderclouds.

Dario lowered his head, though Merle did not miss the hateful look he sent her secretly. "Yes, Master."

"Dario will need a quantity of water. Therefore, you, Merle, will get ten pails full from the well, carry them upstairs, and take them to the workshop. That will be your punishment."

"But Master—," Dario flared.

Arcimboldo cut him short. "You have shamed us all by your behavior, Dario. I know you are rash and hot-tempered, but you are also my best student, and therefore I intend to let it go at this. As far as Merle is concerned, she has only been here for two weeks and must first get used to the fact that here, unlike the orphanage, a dispute is not settled with fists. Have I expressed myself clearly enough?"

Both bowed and said in unison, "Yes, Master."

"Any objections?"

"No, Master."

"So be it." With a wave, he indicated that they could go.

Outside the door of the library Merle and Dario exchanged black looks, then each turned to the appointed task. While Dario prepared to remove the residues of the paint attack in the workshop, Merle ran down into the courtyard. Beside the back door a dozen wooden pails sat lined up. She snatched up the first one and went to the well.

Strange creatures were carved in the stone of the wall around the well, fantastic creatures with cat's eyes, Medusa heads, and reptilian tails. They were strung out in a stiff procession around the well. At their head went a creature, half human, half shark, with arms whose elbows pointed in the wrong direction; in its hands it carried a human head.

The metal lid was heavy. Merle succeeded in opening it only with groaning and straining. Below, there was nothing but blackness. Way deep, deep down, she saw a shimmer of light, the reflection of the sky over the courtyard.

She turned around and looked up. The view was only a little different from the one inside of the well: The walls of the old houses rose up around the courtyard like the stone wall of the well. Perhaps the water wasn't so far down as she'd thought. The reflection of the courtyard added that much more height, and so the well shaft seemed to be more than double its actual length. It would be less trouble to climb down to the surface than Merle had thought—at least now she could see metal handholds going down the inside of the well into the abyss. What could it be that Eft kept doing down there?

Merle tied the bucket to the long rope lying ready beside the well and let it down. The wood scraped against the stone of the wall as it went. The sound reverberated in the depths and rose up distorted into the daylight. Except for Merle there was no one else in the courtyard. The scraping of the bucket was thrown back by the facades of the surrounding houses, and now it almost sounded like whispers murmuring down from the gaping windows of the buildings. The voices of all those who no longer lived here. Ghost whispers.

Merle couldn't see when the bucket reached the surface. It was too dark down there. But she did see that suddenly the reflection of the sky in the depths was set in motion; the bucket was probably just now dipping into the water. Only it was strange that she felt no slackening of the pull and also that the scraping of the bucket on the stone wall sounded unchanged. If it wasn't the bucket that stirred the surface of the water, what was it?

She'd scarcely framed the question when something

appeared down there. A head. It was much too far away for her to be able to make out the details, and yet she was certain that dark eyes were looking up at her.

In her fright Merle let go of the rope and took a step backward. The rope whizzed over the well wall into the depths. It would have been lost, together with the bucket, had not a hand unexpectedly grabbed it.

Eft's hand.

Merle hadn't noticed the housekeeper walking up to her in the courtyard. Eft had grabbed the end of the rope just in time and was now pulling the bucket up into the daylight.

"Thank you," Merle stammered. "That was clumsy of me."

"What did you see?" asked Eft behind her half mask.

"Nothing."

"Please don't lie to me."

Merle hesitated. Eft was still busy pulling up the bucket. Instinctively Merle had a fleeting impulse to turn around and run away. She would have done that a few weeks ago in the orphanage. Here, however, she was reluctant to demean herself. She had done nothing wrong or forbidden.

"There was something down there."

"Oh?"

"A face."

The housekeeper pulled the full bucket over the edge

and placed it on the wall. Water sloshed over the edge and ran down on the grimacing faces of the stone reliefs.

"So, a face. And you are quite sure?" With a sigh Eft answered her own question. "Of course you are."

"I saw it." Merle didn't quite know how she should behave. The housekeeper seemed uncanny to her, but she felt no real fear of her. Rather, a kind of uneasiness at the way she looked over the edge of her mask and seemed to read Merle's thoughts from each movement, each tiny hesitation.

"You've already seen something before, haven't you?" Eft was leaning against the rim of the well. "The other night, for example."

There was no point in lying. "I heard the sound of the cover. And then I saw you climbing into the well."

"Did you tell anyone about it?"

"No," she lied, in order not to draw Junipa into it.

Eft ran her hand through her hair and sighed deeply. "Merle, I have to explain some things to you."

"If you want to."

"You aren't like the other apprentices," said the housekeeper. Was that a smile in her eyes? "Not like Dario. You can handle the truth."

Merle stepped closer to Eft, until she would only have needed to stretch out her hand to touch the mask with the red lips. "You want to trust me with a secret?"

"If you are ready for it."

"But you don't know me at all."

"Perhaps better than you think."

Merle didn't understand what Eft meant by that. Her curiosity was awakened now, and she wondered if that wasn't precisely what Eft intended. The more interested Merle was, the more deeply she would be drawn into the business, and the more Eft could trust her.

"Come with me," the housekeeper said, and she went from the well to the back door of an empty house. The entrance wasn't locked, and after Eft had pushed the door open, they came into a small hallway. Apparently it was the former servants' entrance to the palazzo.

They went past an abandoned kitchen and an empty storeroom, until they came to a short flight of stairs going down—unusual in a city whose houses were built on pilings and only rarely had cellars under them.

A little later Merle realized that Eft had led her to an underground boat landing. A walkway ran alongside a water channel, which disappeared into semicircular tunnels on both sides. At one time goods were loaded onto boats here. It smelled brackish, the air tasted of algae and mold.

"Why don't you go into the water this way?" Merle asked.

"What do you mean?"

"You climb into the well because you want to get somewhere through it. Of course, there could be a secret passageway branching off the well shaft, but I don't believe that. I think that it's the water itself that draws you." She paused briefly and then added, "You're a mermaid, aren't you?"

If Eft was surprised, she didn't show it. Merle understood very well what she was saying—and also how unreasonable it was, basically. Eft had legs, well-shaped human legs, utterly in contrast to all known mermaids, whose hips transmuted into a broad fish tail.

Eft reached both hands behind her head and carefully took down the mask that covered the lower half of her face day and night.

"You aren't afraid of me, are you?" she asked with her broad mouth, whose corners ended a finger's breadth in front of her ears. She had no lips, but when she spoke the folds of skin pulled back and exposed a mouth of several rows of small, sharp teeth.

"No," Merle replied, and it was the truth.

"That's good."

"Will you tell me?"

"What would you like to know?"

"Why you don't take this way here, if you go at night to meet with other mermaids. Why do you run the risk of someone seeing you when you climb into the well?"

Eft's eyes narrowed, which in a human had the effect of an unspoken threat, but with her it was only an expression of distaste. "Because the water is polluted. It's the same in all the canals of the city. It's poisonous, it kills us. That's why so few of us come willingly to Venice. The water of the canals kills us, stealthily, but with absolute certainty."

"The mermaids pulling the boats—"

"Will die. Any of us caught by you humans and caged or misused for your races will die. The poison in the water first corrodes the skin and then the mind. Not even the Flowing Queen can protect us from it."

Merle stood silent with horror. All the people who kept mermaids for fun, like house pets, were murderers. Some might even know what the imprisonment in the canals did to the mermaids.

Ashamed, she looked Eft in the eye. She had trouble bringing out any sound at all. "I've never caught a mermaid."

Eft smiled, showing her needle-sharp teeth. "I know that. I can feel it. You have been touched by the Flowing Queen."

"I?"

"Didn't they fish you out of the water when you were a newborn?"

"You were listening to me and Junipa that first night in our room." With anyone else she would have been indignant, but in Eft's case it didn't seem important.

"I listened," the mermaid admitted. "And because I know your secret, I will reveal mine to you. That's only fair. And so, as I will talk to no one about your secret, you will keep silent about mine."

Merle nodded. "How did you mean that before—that the Flowing Queen has touched me?"

"You were set out on the canals. That happens to many children. But extremely few survive. Most drown. But you were found. The current carried you. That can only mean that the Flowing Queen adopted you."

To Merle's ears it sounded as though Eft had been there, so strong was the conviction resonating in her words. It was obvious that the mermaids revered the Flowing Queen as a goddess. Merle spun the thought further and got goose bumps: What if the Flowing Queen wasn't protecting the people of the lagoon at all? After all, the mermaids were creatures of the water, and if you were to believe some theories, the queen *was* the water. An incomprehensible power of the sea.

"What is the Flowing Queen?" She had no real hope that Eft knew the answer to this question.

"If it was ever known, it's long forgotten," replied the mermaid softly. "The way you and I and the Queen herself will one day be forgotten."

"But the Flowing Queen is revered by all. Everyone in Venice loves her. She has saved us all. No one can ever forget that."

Eft left it with a silent shrug of her shoulders, but Merle was very much aware that she was of a different opinion. The mermaid pointed to a slender gondola lying moored on the black water. It looked as if it were floating in nothing, so smooth and dark was the surface around it.

"Down into that?" Merle asked.

Eft nodded.

"And then?"

"I want to show you something."

"Will we be gone long?"

"An hour at most."

"Arcimboldo will punish me. He told me to take the buckets—"

"Already done." Eft smiled. "He told me what he had in mind for you. I've already put ten full buckets in the workshop."

Merle wasn't convinced. "And Dario?"

"Won't say a word about it. Otherwise Arcimboldo will find out who's swiping his wine at night."

"Then you know about that?"

"Nothing happens in that house without my knowing about it."

Merle hesitated no longer and followed Eft into the gondola. The mermaid loosed the rope, placed herself in the stern of the boat, and steered it with the long oar to one of the two tunnel openings. It became pitch-black around them.

"Don't worry," Eft said, "there's a torch in front of you and there are flints next to it."

It wasn't long before Merle had the pitch of the torch

lit. Yellow and flickering, the firelight flitted over an arching tile ceiling.

"May I ask you something else?"

"You want to know why I have legs and no *kalimar*."

"Kali—what?"

"Kalimar. That's what we call the fish tail in our language."

"Will you tell me?"

Eft let the gondola glide deeper into the darkness of the tunnel. Sheets of moss had loosened from the ceiling and hung down like tattered curtains. It smelled of decaying seaweed and corruption.

"It's a sad story," Eft said finally, "so I'll make it short."

"I like sad stories."

"It could be that you will be the heroine in one yourself." Merle turned to the mermaid and looked at her.

"Why do you say such a thing?" Merle demanded.

"You have been touched by the Flowing Queen," Eft replied, as if that were explanation enough. "Once, a mermaid was washed onto the shore of an island by a storm. She was so weak that she remained lying there, helpless among the rushes. The clouds parted, the sun burned down from the heavens, and the body of the mermaid became dry and brittle and began to die. But then a young man appeared, the son of a trader, whose father had given him the thankless task of trying to trade with the handful of fisherfolk who lived on the island. He'd passed the entire day with the poor families, who'd shared water and fish with him, but they bought nothing, for they had no money and nothing for which it would have paid to trade. Late in the day the merchant's young son was on the way back to his boat, but he didn't dare to face his father after this lack of success. He was afraid of a tongue-lashing, for it wasn't the first time that he'd returned to Venice without success, and even more he feared for his inheritance. His father was a stern, hard-hearted man, who had no understanding of the poverty of the people on the outer islands—really he had no understanding of anything in the world, except making money.

"The young man was now sauntering along the shore of the harbor to put off his return home. As he wandered lost in thought through the reeds and high grass, he stumbled on the stranded mermaid. He knelt down beside her, looked into her eyes, and fell in love with her on the spot. He didn't see the fish tail below her hips, nor did he see the teeth that would have inspired fear in anyone else. He only looked into her eyes, which looked back at him helplessly, and he made up his mind at once: This was the woman he loved and would marry. He carried her back into the water, and while she gradually regained her strength in the billows of the waves, he spoke to her of his love.

The longer she listened to him, the more she liked him.

From liking grew affection, and from affection grew more. They swore to see each other again, and so on the next day they met on the shore of another island, and on the day after that on another, and so it went.

"After several weeks the young man pulled all his courage together and asked if she would follow him to the city. But she knew how it went for mermaids in the city, and so she said no. He promised to make her his wife so that she could live at his side like a human. 'Look at me,' she said, 'I will never be like a human.' And so they were both very sad, and the young man saw that his plan had been nothing but a beautiful dream.

"But the following night the mermaid remembered the legend of a powerful sea witch who lived far out in the Adriatic in an undersea cave. So she swam out, farther than she or any of her companions had ever swum, and found the sea witch sitting on a rock deep in the sea and watching for drowned people. For sea witches, you must know, prize dead meat, and it tastes best to them when it's old and bloated. On the way the mermaid had passed a sunken fishing boat, and so she could bring the witch an especially juicy morsel as a tribute. This put the old one in a gracious mood. She listened to the mermaid's story and decided, probably still intoxicated from the taste of the corpse, to help her. She said a spell and ordered the mermaid to return to the lagoon. There she should lie on a shore of the city and sleep until dawn. Then, the witch promised, she would have legs instead of a tail. 'Only your mouth,' she added, 'that I cannot take from you, for without that you would be silent forever.'

"The mermaid attached no importance to her mouth, for after all, that was part of her face, with which the merchant's son had fallen in love. So she did as the sea witch instructed her.

"On the morning of the next day she was found in a landing place. And in fact, she now had legs where once her fish tail had been. But the men who found her crossed themselves, spoke of the Devil's work, and beat her, for they had recognized her by her mouth for what she really was. The men were convinced that the mermaids had found a way to become human, and they feared that soon they would take over the city, murder all the humans, and steal their wealth.

"What foolishness! As if any mermaid ever cared anything for the riches of humans!

"While the men were beating and kicking her, the mermaid kept whispering the name of her beloved, and so they soon sent for him. He hurried there, in the company of his father, of course, who suspected a conspiracy against him and his house. The mermaid and the young man were brought face-to-face, and both looked into each other's eyes long and deeply. The young man wept, and the mermaid also shed tears, which mixed with the blood on her cheeks. But then her lover turned away, for he was weak and feared his father's anger. 'I don't know her,' he said. 'I have nothing to do with this freak.'

"The mermaid grew very still and said nothing more. She remained silent when they beat her harder, even when the merchant and his son kicked her with their boots in her face and in the ribs. Later they threw her back in the water like a dead fish. They all took her for that too: for dead."

Eft fell silent and for a long moment gripped the oar tightly in her hand, without dipping it in the water. The torchlight shone on her cheeks, and a single tear ran down her face. She wasn't telling the story of some mermaid or other, she was telling her own.

"A child found her, an apprentice in a mirror workshop, whose master had taken him from an orphanage. He took her in, hid her, gave her food and drink, and then kept giving her new spirit when she wanted to put an end to her life. The name of that boy was Arcimboldo, and the mermaid swore in gratitude to follow him her life long. Mermaids live much longer than you humans, and so the boy is an old man today and the mermaid is still young. She will still be young when he dies, and then she will be entirely alone again, a lonely person between two worlds, no longer a mermaid and also not a human."

When Merle looked up at her, the tears on Eft's cheeks had dried. Now it seemed again as if she had told someone else's story, someone whose fate was distant and unmeaning.

Merle would have liked to stand up and throw her arms around her, but she knew that Eft didn't expect it and also wouldn't have wanted it.

"Only a story," whispered the mermaid. "As true and as untrue as all the others that we would rather never have heard."

"I'm glad you told me."

Eft nodded slightly, then looked up and pointed forward beyond Merle. "Look," she said, "we're there."

The torchlight around them paled, although the flame still burned. It took a moment for Merle to realize that the walls of the tunnel were behind them. The gondola had glided soundlessly into an underground hall or cave.

Ahead of them an incline rose out of the darkness. It ascended as a steep slope out of the water and was covered with something that Merle couldn't make out from a distance. Plants perhaps. A pale, intertwined branching. But what plant of that size could thrive here underground?

Once, while they were crossing the dark sea that was the floor of the hall, she thought she saw movement in the water. She told herself that they were fish. Very large fish.

"There's no mountain around here," she said, voicing her thoughts. "So how can there be a cave in the middle of Venice?" She knew enough about the behavior of reflections to be sure that they could not be *under* the sea. Whatever this hall was, it was located in the city, among splendid palazzi and elegant building facades—and it had been artificially constructed.

"Who built this?" she asked.

"A friend of the mermaids." Eft's tone indicated that she didn't intend to speak about it.

Such a place in the middle of the city! If it actually was located above ground it must have an outside. What was it camouflaged as? A decaying palazzo of a long-forgotten noble family? A huge warehouse? There were no windows to give access to the outside, and in the darkness neither the ceiling nor the side walls were discernible, only the strange incline, which came closer and closer.

Merle realized now that her first doubts had been right. There were no plants growing on the incline. The branching structure was something else.

Her heart suddenly missed a beat as she realized the truth.

It was bones. The bones of hundreds of mermaids. Twining over and under and into one another, forged together by death, aslant and in a jumble. With racing heart she saw that the upper bodies looked like human ribs, while the fish tail resembled a supergigantic fish bone. The sight was as absurd as it was shocking.

"They all came here to die?"

"Of their own free will, yes," said Eft as she steered the gondola to the left so that the starboard side faced the mountain of bones.

The torchlight gave the illusion of movement in the branched bones where none was. The thin shadows twitched and trembled, they moved like spider legs that had been detached from their bodies and now were flitting among one another on their own.

"The mermaids' cemetery," Merle whispered. Everyone knew the old legend. The cemetery had been thought to be far out on the edge of the lagoon or on the high sea. Treasure-seekers and knights of fortune had tried to track it down, for the bones of a mermaid were more precious than elephant tusk, harder, and in olden days they were feared as weapons in the battles of man against man. That the cemetery lay in the city, under the eyes of all the inhabitants, was hard to grasp—and in addition, that a human must have helped to establish it. What had prompted him to do it? And who had he been?

"I wanted you to see this place." Eft bowed slightly, and only after a moment was it clear to Merle that the gesture was meant for her. "Secret for secret. Silence for all time. And the oath upon it of one who has been touched."

"I should swear?"

Eft nodded.

Merle didn't know how else to do it, so she raised a hand and said solemnly, "I swear an oath on my life that I will never tell anyone of the mermaids' cemetery."

"The oath as one who has been touched," Eft demanded.

"I, Merle, who was touched by the Flowing Queen, swear this oath."

Eft nodded, satisfied, and Merle gave a sigh of relief.

The hull of the gondola scraped over something that lay under the surface of the water.

"Still more bones," Eft explained. "Thousands." She turned the gondola and sculled back in the direction of the tunnel entrance.

"Eft?"

"Hmm?"

"You really think I'm something special, don't you?"

The mermaid smiled mysteriously. "That you certainly are. Something very special."

Much later, in the dark, in bed, Merle slipped her arm into the water mirror under the bedclothes, enjoyed the comfortable warmth, and felt for the hand on the other side. It took a while, but then something touched her fingers, very gentle, very reassuring. Merle sighed softly and fell into a restless half sleep.

Outside the window the evening star rose. Its twinkling was reflected in Junipa's open mirror eyes, which stared, cold and glassy, across the dark room.

4

PHANTOMS

"HAVE YOU EVER LOOKED INTO IT?" JUNIPA ASKED NEXT morning, after they'd awakened to the sound of Eft's ringing the gong in the hallway.

Merle rubbed the sleep from her eyes with the knuckle of her index finger. "Into what?"

"Into your water mirror."

"Oh, sure. All the time."

Junipa swung her legs over the edge of the bed and looked at Merle. Her mirror fragments flared golden from the sunrise behind the roofs.

"I don't mean just looked in."

"Behind the water surface?"

Junipa nodded. "Have you?"

"Two or three times," Merle said. "I've pushed my face in as far as possible. The frame is pretty narrow, but it worked. My eyes were underwater."

"And?"

"Nothing. Just darkness."

"You couldn't see anything at all?"

"I just said that."

Thoughtfully Junipa ran her fingers through her hair. "If you want, I'll try it."

Merle, who was just about to yawn, snapped her mouth shut again. "You?"

"With the mirror eyes I can see in the dark."

Merle raised her eyebrows. "You didn't tell me about that at all." She hastily considered whether she'd done anything at night to be ashamed of.

"It just began three days ago. But now it's getting stronger from night to night. I see the same as by daylight. Sometimes I can't sleep because the brightness even penetrates my eyelids. Then everything gets red, as if you were looking at the bright sun with your eyes closed."

"You have to talk with Arcimboldo about that."

Junipa looked unhappy. "And what if he takes the mirrors away from me?"

"He would never do that." Concerned, Merle tried to imagine what it would be like to be surrounded by light day and night. What if it got worse? Could Junipa sleep at all then?

"So," Junipa quickly changed the subject, "how about it? Shall I try it?"

Merle pulled the hand mirror out from under the covers, weighed it in her hand for a moment, then shrugged her shoulders. "Why not?"

Junipa climbed up beside her on the bed. They sat opposite each other, cross-legged. Their nightshirts stretched across their knees and both were still tousle-headed from sleep.

"Let me try it first," Merle said.

Junipa watched as Merle brought the mirror right up to her eyes. Carefully she dipped her nose in, then—as far as possible—the rest of her face. Soon the frame was pressed against her cheekbones. She could go no deeper.

Merle opened her eyes underwater. She knew what to expect, so she wasn't disappointed. It was the same as always. Nothing but darkness.

She removed the mirror from her face. The water remained trapped in the frame, not the finest trace of dampness gleaming on her skin.

"And?" Junipa asked excitedly.

"Nothing at all." Merle handed her the mirror. "As usual."

Junipa gripped the handle in her narrow hand. She

looked at the reflecting surface and studied her new eyes. "Do you really think they're pretty?" she asked suddenly.

Merle hesitated. "Unusual."

"That's no answer to my question."

"I'm sorry." Merle wished that Junipa had spared herself the truth. "Sometimes I get goose bumps when I look at you. Not because your eyes are ugly," she added quickly. "They are just so . . . so . . ."

"They feel cold," said Junipa softly, as if she were deep in thought. "Sometimes I feel cold, even when the sun is shining."

Brightness at night, cold in the sunshine.

"Do you really want to do it?" Merle asked. She remembered how reluctant Junipa had been to put her hand in the mirror; how the water had felt ice-cold to her.

"Really, I don't want to, I know that already," Junipa said. "But if you say so, I'll try it for you." She looked at Merle. "Wouldn't you like to know what's back there, where the hand comes from?"

Merle only nodded mutely.

Junipa pushed the mirror up to her face and dipped it in. Her head was smaller than Merle's—as all of her was more petite, slender, vulnerable—and so it vanished up to the temples in the water.

Merle waited. She observed Junipa's thin body under the much-too-large nightshirt, the way her shoulders stuck out underneath it and her collarbones protruded over the edge of the neckline, outlined as sharply as if they lay over the skin instead of under it.

The sight was strange, almost a little mad, now that for the first time she was seeing another person working with the mirror. Mad things could be quite normal, so long as you were doing them yourself. Watching someone else doing them, you wrinkled your nose, turned around quickly, and walked away.

But Merle kept on watching, and she wondered what it was that Junipa was seeing at that moment.

Finally she couldn't stand it any longer and asked, "Junipa? Can you hear me?"

Of course she could. Her ears were above the surface of the water. But all the same, she didn't answer.

"Junipa?"

Merle was uneasy, but she still didn't interfere. Very slowly visions welled up in her, pictures of beasts that were gnawing on her friend's face on the other side. Now, when she pulled her head back, it would just be a hollow shell of bone and hair, like the helmets of the tribes that Professor Burbridge had discovered during his expedition to Hell.

"Junipa?" she asked again, this time a bit more sharply. She grasped her friend's free hand. Her skin was warm. Merle could feel the pulse.

Junipa returned. It was just exactly that: a return. Her face had the expression of a person who has been very far away, in distant, inconceivable lands, which perhaps existed on the other side of the globe or only in her imagination.

"What was there?" Merle asked uneasily. "What did you see?"

She would have given a lot if Junipa at this moment had had the eyes of a human. Eyes in which a person could read something—sometimes things you might rather not have known, but always the truth.

But Junipa's eyes remained blank and hard and without any feeling.

Can she still cry? ran through Merle's mind, and at the moment the question seemed more important than any other.

However, Junipa was not crying. Only the corners of her mouth twitched. But it didn't look as though she wanted to smile.

Merle bent toward her, took the mirror out of her hand, laid it on the covers, and gently grasped her by the shoulders. "What *is* in the mirror?"

Junipa was silent for a moment, then silvery glass turned in Merle's direction. "It's dark over there."

I know that, Merle wanted to say, before it became clear to her that Junipa meant a different darkness from the one Merle had seen.

"Tell me about it," she demanded.

Junipa shook her head. "No. You can't ask me about it."

"What?" Merle cried.

Junipa shrugged Merle off and stood up. "Never ask me what I saw there," she said tonelessly. "Never."

"But Junipa—"

"Please."

"It can't be anything bad!" cried Merle. Defiance and despair welled up in her. "I've felt the hand. The hand, Junipa!"

Outside the window a cloud moved in front of the morning sun, and Junipa's mirror eyes also darkened. "Let it be, Merle. Forget the hand. Best forget the mirror altogether." With these words she turned, opened the door, and walked out into the hall.

Merle sat transfixed on the bed, incapable of thinking clearly. She heard the door slam, and then she felt herself very alone.

That same day, Arcimboldo sent his two girl students on the hunt for mirror phantoms.

"I want to show you something quite unusual today," he said in the afternoon. Out of the corner of her eye Merle saw Dario and the other two boys exchange looks and grin.

The master mirror maker pointed to the door that led to the storeroom behind the workshop. "You haven't been in there yet," he said. "And for good reason."

Merle had assumed he was afraid for his finished magic mirrors, which were stored there.

"The handling of the mirrors as I produce them is not entirely without danger." Arcimboldo leaned with both hands on the workbench behind him. "Now and again one must clear them of certain"—he hesitated—"of certain elements."

Again the three boys grinned, and Merle slowly became angry. She hated it when Dario knew more than she did.

"Dario and the others stay here in the workshop," said Arcimboldo. "Junipa and Merle, you come with me."

Then he turned and went to the door of the storeroom. Merle and Junipa exchanged looks, then followed him.

"Good luck," said Boro. It sounded sincere.

"Good luck," mimicked Dario and murmured something after it that Merle didn't catch.

Arcimboldo let the girls in and then closed the door after them. "Welcome into the heart of my house," he said.

The sight he presented to them warranted the ceremony of his words.

It was hard to say how big the room was. Its walls were covered over and over with mirrors, and rows of mirrors also stretched down its center, placed behind one another like dominoes just before they are knocked down. Sunlight shone in through a glass ceiling—the workshop was in an addition that wasn't nearly so high as the rest of the house.

The mirrors were secured with braces and chains that

anchored them to the walls. Nothing would topple here, if Venice were to be struck by an earthquake or if Hell itself were to open under the city—as it was said to have done under Marrakesh, a city in North Africa. But that had been more than thirty years before, right after the outbreak of the war. Today no one talked about Marrakesh. It had vanished from the maps and the language of men.

"How many mirrors are there?" asked Junipa.

It was impossible to estimate their number, to say nothing of counting them. They reflected each other again and again in their glassy surfaces, mutually adding and multiplying themselves. Merle had a thought: Was a mirror that existed only in a mirror not just as real as its original? It fulfilled its role just as well as its counterpart—it reflected.

Merle couldn't think of anything else that was able to do this: to do something without itself being. For the first time, she asked herself whether all mirrors were not always magic mirrors. *Mirrors can see,* Arcimboldo had said. Now she believed him.

"You are now going to make the acquaintance of a very singular kind of nuisance," he explained. "My special friends—the mirror phantoms."

"Mirror phantoms? What are they?" Junipa spoke softly, almost fearfully, as though the images of what she had seen behind Merle's water mirror still danced before her eyes and made her afraid.

Arcimboldo stepped in front of the first mirror in the

center row. It reached almost to his chin. Its frame was of plain wood, like the frames of all the mirrors from Arcimboldo's workshop. They not only served as ornament but also prevented cut fingers during transport.

"Just look in," he demanded.

The girls walked to his side and stared at the mirror. Junipa noticed it first. "There's something in the glass."

It looked like shreds of mist that moved fleetingly over the mirror surface, amorphous, like ghosts. And there was no doubt that the pale outline was *under* the glass, inside the mirror.

"Mirror phantoms," said Arcimboldo matter-of-factly. "Annoying parasites who settle into my mirrors from time to time. It's the apprentices' job to catch them."

"And how are we supposed to do that?" Merle wanted to know.

"You'll enter the mirrors and drive out the phantoms with a little aid that I shall give you to take with you." He laughed aloud. "My goodness, don't look so flabbergasted! Dario and the others have done it countless times. It may seem a little unusual to you, but basically it's not very difficult. Just tiresome. Therefore, you apprentices are allowed to experience it, while your old master puts his feet on the desk, smokes a good pipe, and doesn't worry about a thing."

Merle and Junipa exchanged looks. They both felt apprehensive, but they were also determined to get through this business with dignity. After all, if Dario had already done it, they probably would be able to as well.

Arcimboldo pulled something out of a pocket of his smock. Between thumb and forefinger he held it in front of the girls' noses: a transparent glass ball, no bigger than Merle's fist.

"Quite ordinary, eh?" Arcimboldo grinned, and for the first time, Merle noticed that he was missing a tooth. "But in fact, it's the best weapon against mirror phantoms. Unfortunately, it's also the only one."

He said nothing for a moment, but neither girl asked any questions. Merle was certain that Arcimboldo would carry on with his explanation.

After a short pause, while he gave them a chance to look at the glass ball more closely, he said, "A glassblower on Murano produced this captivating little thing according to my specifications."

Specifications? Merle asked herself. *For a simple ball of glass?*

"When you put it next to a mirror phantom, you must just speak a certain word, and he'll immediately be trapped inside the ball," Arcimboldo explained. "The word is *intorabiliuspeteris.* You must imprint it in your minds as if it were your own name. Intorabiliuspeteris."

The girls repeated the strange word, becoming tongue-tangled a few times, until they were sure they could keep it in their heads.

The master pulled out a second ball, handed one to each girl, and had them step up to the mirror. "Several mirrors are infested, but for today we'll let it go with one." He made a sort of bow in the direction of the mirror and spoke a word in a strange language.

"Enter," he said then.

"Just like that?" Merle asked.

Arcimboldo laughed. "Of course. Or would you rather ride in on a horse?"

Merle ran her eye over the mirror surface. It looked smooth and solid, not yielding like her hand mirror. The memory made her briefly look over at Junipa. Whatever she'd seen this morning, it had made a deep impression on her. Now she seemed to be afraid to follow Arcimboldo's instructions. For a moment Merle was tempted to tell the master everything and ask for understanding for Junipa to remain here and Merle to go alone.

But then Junipa took the first step and stretched out her hand. Her fingers broke through the mirror surface like the skin on a pan of boiled milk. She quickly looked over her shoulder at Merle; then, with a strained smile, she stepped inside the mirror. Her figure was still recognizable, but now it looked flat and somehow *unreal,* like a figure in a painting. She waved to Merle.

"Brave girl," murmured Arcimboldo with satisfaction.

Merle broke through the mirror surface with a single

step. She felt a cold tickling, like a gentle breeze at midnight, then she was on the other side and looking around.

She had once heard of a mirror labyrinth that was supposed to have been in a palazzo on the Campo Santa Maria Nova. She knew no one who had seen it with his own eyes, but the pictures that the stories had conjured up in her mind bore no comparison with what she now saw before her.

One thing was clear at first glance: The mirror world was a kingdom of deceptions. It was the place under the double bottom of the kaleidoscope, the robbers' cave in the *Tales from a Thousand and One Nights,* the palace of the gods on Olympus. It was artificial, an illusion, a dream dreamed only by those who believed in it. And yet at this moment it seemed as substantial as Merle herself. Did the figures in a painting also think they were in a real place? Prisoners who were not aware of their imprisonment?

Before them lay a room of mirrors: not like Arcimboldo's storeroom, much more a structure that from top to bottom, from left to right, consisted of mirrors and mirrors alone. Yet the first impression was deceptive. If you took a step forward, you bumped up against an invisible glass wall, while there, where the end of the room appeared to be, was nothing but emptiness, followed by other mirrors, invisible connecting passageways, and fresh deceptions.

It took a moment for Merle to realize what was really troubling about this place: The mirrors reflected only each other, not the two girls who were standing in their middle. So it happened that they could walk straight up to a mirror and bump against it without being warned by their own reflection. On all sides, the mirrors reflected themselves to infinity, a world of silver and crystal.

Merle and Junipa made several attempts to move deeper into the labyrinth, but again and again they bumped against glass.

"This is pointless," Merle protested and stamped her foot in anger. Mirror glass creaked under her foot without splintering.

"They're all around us," Junipa whispered.

"The phantoms?"

Junipa nodded.

Merle looked around. "I can't see any."

"They're afraid. My eyes scare them. They're avoiding us."

Merle turned around. There was a sort of door at the place where they'd entered the mirror world. There she thought she could perceive a movement, but perhaps that was only Arcimboldo, waiting for them in the real world.

Something whisked past her face, a pale flicker. Two arms, two legs, a head. Close up, it no longer looked like a patch of fog but rather like the blur caused by a drop of water in the eye.

Merle raised the glass ball, feeling a little foolish. "Intorabiliuspeteris," she cried, and immediately felt even more foolish.

There was the sound of a soft sigh, then the phantom shot right at her. The ball sucked him to its inside, which soon flickered and grew streaky, as if it were filled with a white, oily fluid.

"It works!" Merle gasped.

Junipa nodded but made no attempt to use her own ball. "Now they're terribly afraid."

"You can really see them all around us?"

"Very clearly."

It must have to do with Junipa's eyes, with the magic of the mirror pieces. Now Merle also saw other blurs at the edge of her vision, but she couldn't make out the phantoms as clearly as Junipa seemed to be able to.

"If they're afraid, that means that they're living beings," she said, thinking aloud.

"Yes," Junipa said. "But it's as if they weren't really here. As if they were only a part of themselves, like a shadow that's separated from its owner."

"Then perhaps it's a good thing if we get them out of here. Perhaps they're prisoners here."

"Do you think in the glass ball they aren't?"

Of course Junipa was right. But Merle wanted to get back into the real world as fast as possible, away from this glassy labyrinth. Arcimboldo would only be satisfied when they'd caught all the phantoms. She was afraid otherwise he'd send them right back into the mirror.

She no longer paid any attention to what Junipa was doing. Merle stretched out her arm with the ball, waved it in different directions, and called the magic word over and over: "Intorabiliuspeteris . . . intorabiliuspeteris . . . intorabiliuspeteris!"

The hissing and whistling became louder and sharper, and at the same time the ball filled with the swirling fog until it looked as if the glass were being steamed up on the inside. Once, in the orphanage, one of the attendants had blown cigar smoke into a wine glass, and the effect had been very similar: The layers of smoke had rotated behind the glass as though there were something living inside trying to get out.

What sort of creatures were these that infested Arcimboldo's magic mirrors like aphids in a vegetable garden? Merle would have loved to know more.

Junipa was grasping her ball so tightly in her fist that it suddenly cracked and shattered in her hand. Tiny splinters of glass rained onto the mirror floor, followed by dark drops of blood, as the sharp edges cut into Junipa's fingers.

"Junipa!" Merle stuffed her ball into her pocket, sprang to Junipa's side, and anxiously examined her hand. "Oh, Junipa . . ." She slipped out of her sweater and wrapped it around her friend's forearm. That made visible the upper edge of the hand mirror, stuck into her dress pocket.

Suddenly one of the phantoms whizzed in a narrow spiral around her upper body and disappeared into the surface of the water mirror.

"Oh, no," Junipa said tearfully, "that's all my fault."

Merle was more concerned about Junipa's well-being than about the mirror. "I think we've caught all of them anyway," she said, unable to take her eyes from the blood on the floor. Her face was mirrored in the drops, as if the blood had tiny eyes that were looking up at her. "Let's get out of here."

Junipa held her back. "Are you going to tell Arcimboldo one of them went—"

Merle interrupted her. "No, he'd just take it away from me."

Stricken, Junipa nodded, and Merle reassuringly laid an arm around her shoulders. "Don't give it another thought."

She gently urged Junipa back to the door, a glittering rectangle not far from them. Arms tightly wrapped around one another, they walked out of the mirror into the storeroom.

"What happened?" asked Arcimboldo, when he saw the wrapping around Junipa's hand. Immediately he unwrapped it, discovered the cuts, and ran to the door. "Eft!" he bellowed out into the workroom. "Bring bandages. Quickly!"

Merle also appraised the cuts. Happily, none of them

seemed to be really dangerous. Most of them weren't very deep, just red scratches on which very thin clots were already forming.

Junipa pointed to the blood spots on Merle's wadded-up sweater. "I'll wash that for you."

"Eft can take care of that," Arcimboldo interposed. "Instead, tell me how this happened!"

Merle told in a few words what had occurred. Only, she kept to herself the flight of the last phantom into her hand mirror. "I caught all the phantoms," she said, pulling the ball out of her pocket. The bright streaks in its interior were now rotating hectically.

Arcimboldo grasped the ball and held it up to the light. What he saw seemed to please him, for he nodded in satisfaction. "You did very well," he praised the two girls. Not a word about the broken ball.

"Now rest," he advised them after Eft had treated the cuts. Then he waved to Dario, Boro, and Tiziano, who'd been lurking at the storeroom door. "You three take care of the rest."

As Merle was leaving the workshop with Junipa, she turned once more to Arcimboldo. "What happens to them now?" She pointed to the ball in the master's hand.

"We throw them into the canal," he replied with a shrug. "Let them settle into the reflections on the water."

Merle nodded, as if she'd expected nothing else, then led Junipa up to their room.

The news spread around the workshop like wildfire. There was going to be a festival! Tomorrow it would be thirty-six years to the day since the army hosts of the Egyptian Empire were massed at the edges of the lagoon. Steamboats and galleys had crossed the water and sunbarks were standing ready in the skies for the attack on the helpless city. But the Flowing Queen had protected Venice, and since then this day had been celebrated throughout the entire city with festivals of rejoicing. One of them would be taking place very close by. Tiziano had heard about it that morning when he went with Eft to the fish market, and he immediately told Dario, who told Boro and, a little reluctantly, passed it on to Merle and Junipa.

"A festival in honor of the Flowing Queen! Right around the corner! There'll be lanterns up everywhere and beer barrels tapped and wine corks popping!"

"Something for you children too?" Arcimboldo, who'd been listening, wore a sly smile as he spoke.

"We aren't children anymore!" flared Dario. Then, with a scornful sideways glance at Junipa, he added, "At least most of us."

Merle was about to leap to Junipa's defense, but it wasn't necessary. "If it's an expression of adulthood," Junipa said with unwonted pertness, "to pick your nose at night, scratch your behind, and do lots of other things, then you're of course *very* grown-up. Right, Dario?"

Dario turned scarlet at her words. But Merle stared at her friend in amazement. Had Junipa slipped into the boys' room at night and observed them? Or could she, thanks to her new mirror eyes, even see through walls? This thought made Merle feel uncomfortable.

Dario was swelling with indignation, but Arcimboldo settled the argument with a wave. "Settle down now, or none of you will go to the festival! On the other hand, if you've finished your jobs punctually by sundown tomorrow, I see no reason—"

The rest of his words were lost in the cries of the apprentices. Even Junipa was beaming all over. It looked as though a shadow had lifted from her features.

"However, one thing you should all keep in mind," said the master. "The students from the weaving workshop will assuredly be there. I want no trouble. Bad enough that our canal has become a battlefield. I will not permit this quarrel to be carried elsewhere. We've already drawn enough attention to ourselves. So—no insults, no fighting, not even a crooked look." His eyes singled out Dario from the other apprentices. "Understand?"

Dario took a deep breath and nodded hastily. The others hastened to murmur their agreement as well. Actually, Merle was grateful for Arcimboldo's words, for the last thing she wanted was a new scrap with the weaver boys. Junipa's wounds had been healing well over the last three days; she needed some peace now to heal completely.

"Now, then, all back to work," the master said, satisfied.

To Merle the time till the festival seemed endless. She was excited and could hardly wait to be among people again, not because she'd had enough of the workshop and its inhabitants—Dario being the one exception—but because she missed the untamed life in the streets, the chattering voices of the women and the transparent boastings of the men.

Finally the evening arrived, and they all left the house together. The boys ran ahead, while Merle and Junipa followed slowly. Arcimboldo had made a pair of glasses for Junipa with dark glass that was supposed to keep anyone from noticing her mirror eyes.

The small troop turned the corner where the Canal of the Expelled opened into the wider waterway. Even from afar they could see hundreds of lanterns on the house fronts, lights in the windows and doors. A small bridge, hardly more than a pedestrian crossing, linked their side to that place. Its railings were decorated with lanterns and candles, while the people sat on the sidewalks, some on stools and chairs they'd brought out of their houses, others on cushions or on the bare stone. In several places drinks were being sold, although Merle realized with a trace of malicious pleasure that Dario was sure to be disappointed: There was hardly any wine or beer, for this was a poor people's festival. No one here could afford to pay fantastic sums for grapes or barley, which had to be smuggled into the city by dangerous routes. After all these years, the Pharaoh's siege ring was just as tight as at the beginning of the war. Even though the siege was imperceptible in daily life, still no one doubted that hardly a mouse, not to mention a smugglers' boat, could sneak past the Egyptian army camps. One could certainly find wine—as Arcimboldo did—but it was usually difficult, even dangerous. The poor people drank water ordinarily, while at festivals they had to be content with juices and various home-distilled liquors of fruits and vegetables.

Up on the bridge, Merle saw the weaver's apprentice who'd been the first to lose his mask. There were two other boys with him. One's face was very red, as if he were sunburned; clearly it hadn't been easy for him to wash off the glue Merle had sprayed under his mask.

Their leader, Serafin, was nowhere to be seen. Merle realized with surprise that she'd involuntarily been watching for him and was almost disappointed not to see him.

Junipa, on the other hand, was a completely changed girl. She couldn't get over her amazement. She kept whispering to Merle, "See him over there?" and "Oh, look at her!" and giggling and laughing, occasionally so loudly that some people turned around and looked at them in surprise and were especially interested at the sight of her dark glasses. Only the rich dandies usually wore such things, and they rarely mixed with the common people. On the other hand, Junipa's worn dress left no doubt about the fact that she had never seen the inside of a palazzo.

The two girls stood at the left end of the bridge and sipped at their juice, which had been watered down too much. On the other side a fiddler was striking up a dance; soon a flute player joined in. The dresses of the young girls whirled like colored tops.

"You're so quiet," Junipa declared, not knowing where to look next. Merle had never seen her so animated. She was glad, for she'd been afraid all the hurly-burly might make Junipa anxious.

"You're looking for that boy." Junipa gave her a silvery look over the top of her glasses. "Serafin."

"Where'd you get that idea?"

"I was blind for thirteen years. I know people. When people know you don't see, they get careless. They mix up blindness with deafness. You just have to listen and they tell you everything about themselves."

"And what have I betrayed about myself?" Merle asked, frowning.

Junipa laughed. "I can see you now, and that's enough. You're looking in all directions all the time. And who could you be looking for except Serafin?"

"You're just imagining that."

"No, I'm not."

"You are so."

Junipa's laugh rang bright and clear. "I'm your friend, Merle. Girls *talk* about a thing like that."

Merle made a move as if to hit her, and Junipa giggled like a child. "Oh, leave me alone," cried Merle, laughing.

Junipa looked up. "There he is, over there."

"Where?"

"There, on the other side."

Junipa was right. Serafin was sitting a little back from the edge of the pavement and letting his legs dangle over the canal. The soles of his shoes were dangerously close to the water.

"Now, go on over to him," Junipa said.

"Not on your life."

"Why ever not?"

"He *is* a weaver apprentice, after all. One of our enemies, or have you forgotten already? I can't just . . . it's bad manners."

"It's even worse manners to act as if you're listening to a friend when in fact your thoughts are somewhere else entirely."

"Can you also read thoughts with those eyes of yours?" asked Merle with amusement.

Junipa shook her head earnestly, as if she'd actually taken the possibility into consideration. "A person just has to look at you."

"You really think I should talk to him?"

"Certainly." Junipa grinned. "Or are you a little afraid?"

"Nonsense. I really just want to ask him how long he's worked for Umberto," Merle said.

"*Very* poor excuse!"

"Ninny!—No, you aren't. You're a treasure!" And with that Merle grabbed Junipa around the neck, hugged her briefly, and then ran across the bridge to the other side. As she went, she looked back over her shoulder and saw Junipa looking after her with a gentle smile.

"Hello."

Shocked, Merle stopped in her tracks. Serafin must have seen her, for suddenly he was standing directly in front of her.

"Hello," she replied, sounding as though she'd just swallowed a fruit pit. "You here too?"

"Looks like it."

"I thought you were probably home hatching plans for splashing paint in other people's faces."

"Oh, that. . . ." He grinned. "We don't do that every day. Would you like something to drink?"

She'd left her cup beside Junipa, so she nodded. "Juice. Please."

Serafin turned and walked to a stand. Merle watched him from the back. He was a handsbreadth taller than she, somewhat thin, perhaps, but so were they all. After all, anyone born during siege conditions never had the embarrassment of having to worry about his weight. Unless you were rich, of course. Or, she thought cynically, you were named Ruggiero and secretly ate up half the orphanage kitchen.

Serafin came back and handed her a wooden cup. "Apple juice," he said. "I hope you like it."

To be polite, she immediately took a sip. "Yes, very much, in fact."

"You're new at Arcimboldo's, aren't you?"

"You know that very well." She immediately regretted her words. Why was she being so snippy? Couldn't she give him a normal answer? "Since a few weeks ago," she added.

"Were you and your friend in the same orphanage?"

She shook her head. "Uh-uh."

"Arcimboldo did something to her eyes."

"She was blind. Now Junipa can see."

"Then it's true, what Master Umberto said."

"And that was?"

"He said Arcimboldo knows his way around magic."

"That's what others say about Umberto."

Serafin grinned. "I've now been in his house for more than two years, and he's never showed me a single magic trick."

"I think Arcimboldo will keep that to himself till the bitter end too."

They laughed a little nervously, not because they'd discovered their first thing in common, but because neither one knew quite how to take the conversation further.

"Shall we walk on a little bit?" Serafin pointed down the canal where the crowds of people were thinner and the lanterns shone on empty water.

Merle grinned mischievously. "It's a good thing we don't belong to fine society. Otherwise it would be improper, wouldn't it?"

"I don't give a hoot about fine society."

"Thing in common number two."

Close beside each other, but without touching, they ambled along the canal. The music became softer and soon was left behind them. The water lapped rhythmically against the dark walls. Somewhere over them pigeons cooed in the niches and carvings of the houses. They turned a corner and left the light of the shoals of lanterns.

"Have you had to chase mirror spirits yet?" Serafin asked after a while.

"Spirits? Do you think it's spirits living in the mirrors?"

"Master Umberto said it's the spirits of all the people Arcimboldo's cheated."

Merle laughed. "And you believe that?"

"No," Serafin replied seriously, "because I know better."

"But you're a weaver, not a mirror maker."

"I've only been a weaver for two years. Before, I was sometimes here, sometimes there, all over Venice."

"Have you still got parents?"

"Not that I know of. At least they've never introduced themselves to me."

"But you weren't in an orphanage too?"

"No. I lived on the street. As I said, sometimes here, sometimes there. And during that time I picked up a lot of stuff. Things that not everybody knows."

"Like how to clean a rat before you eat it?" she asked derisively.

He made a face. "That, too, yes. But I didn't mean that."

A black cat whisked past them, then made a turn and came back. Without warning it leaped onto Serafin. But it wasn't an attack. Instead it landed purposefully on Serafin's shoulder and purred. Serafin didn't even jump but raised his hand and began to stroke the animal.

"You're a thief!" Merle burst out. "Only thieves are so friendly with cats."

"Strays together," he confirmed with a smile. "Thieves and cats have much in common. And share so much with each other." He sighed. "But you're right. I grew up among thieves. At five I became a member of the Guild, then later one of its masters."

"A master thief!" Merle was dumbfounded. The master thieves of the Guild were the most skillful pilferers in Venice. "But you aren't more than fifteen years old!"

He nodded. "At thirteen I left the Guild and went into the service of Umberto. He could well use someone like me. Someone who can climb through ladies' windows on the sly at night and deliver them the goods they've ordered. You probably know that most husbands aren't happy to see their wives doing business with Umberto. His reputation is—"

"Bad?"

"Oh, well, more or less. But his clothes make them slender. And very few women want their husbands to learn how much plumper they actually are. Umberto's reputation may not be the best, but his business is doing better than ever."

"The husbands will find out the truth, at least when their wives . . ." Merle blushed. "When they get undressed."

"Oh, there are tricks and dodges there, too. They turn off the light, or they make their husbands drunk. Women are cleverer than you think."

"I *am* a woman!"

"In a few years, maybe."

She stopped indignantly. "Serafin Master Thief, I don't think that you know enough about women—aside from where they hide their purses—to express yourself about such things."

The black cat on Serafin's shoulder spat at Merle, but she didn't care about that. Serafin whispered something into the cat's ear and it calmed down at once.

"I didn't mean to insult you." He seemed quite taken aback by Merle's outburst. "Really, I didn't."

She gave him a piercing look. "Well, then I'll excuse you this one time."

He bowed, so that the cat had to dig her claws firmly into his shirt. "My most humble thanks, madam."

Merle looked away quickly to hide her smile. When she looked at him again, the cat had vanished. Spots of red blood showed through the fabric of Serafin's shirt where its claws had dug into his shoulder.

"That must hurt," she said with concern.

"Which is more painful? Being scratched by an animal or by a human?"

She chose not to answer that. Instead she walked on, and again Serafin was right next to her.

"You were going to tell me something about the mirror phantoms," she said.

"Was I?"

"You ought not to have started about it otherwise."

Serafin nodded. "You're right. It's only—" He stopped speaking suddenly, stood still, and listened into the night.

"What is it?"

"Shh," he said, and gently laid a finger on her lips.

She strained to hear in the darkness. In the narrow alleys and canals of Venice you often heard the strangest noises. The close spacing between houses distorted sounds beyond recognition. The twisting labyrinths of alleyways were empty after dark because most people preferred to use busier main ways. Robbers and assassins made many districts unsafe, and usually cries, whimpers, or rushing footsteps rebounded from the old walls and were transmitted as echoes to places that lay far from the source of the sound. If Serafin had in fact heard something to arouse concern, it might mean everything or nothing: The danger could be lurking around the next corner, but it also might be many hundreds of yards away.

"Soldiers!" he hissed. He grabbed the surprised Merle by the arm and pulled her into one of the narrow tunnels that ran between many houses in the city, built-over alleyways in which utter darkness reigned at night.

"Are you sure?" she whispered very close to his cheek, and she felt him nod.

"Two men on lions. Around the corner."

At that moment they saw the two of them, in uniform, with sword and rifle, riding on gray basalt lions. The lions bore their riders past the mouth of the passageway with majestic steps. It was astonishing with what grace the lions moved. Their bodies were of massive stone and nevertheless they glided like lithe house cats. Their claws, sharp as daggers, scraped over the pavement and left deep furrows.

When the patrol was far enough away, Serafin whispered, "Some of them know my face. So I'm not keen to meet them."

"Anyone who was already a master thief at thirteen certainly has reason for that."

He smiled, flattered. "Could be."

"Why did you leave the Guild?"

"The older masters couldn't stand it that I made bigger hauls than they did. They spread lies about me and tried to get me thrown out of the Guild. So I chose to leave voluntarily." He walked out of the passageway into the pale shine of a gas lantern. "But come on—I promised to tell you more about the mirror phantoms. To do that, I have to show you something first."

5

TREACHERY

MERLE AND SERAFIN WALKED FARTHER THROUGH THE
maze of narrow alleys and passages, here turning right,
there left, crossing bridges over still canals, and going
through gateways and along under clotheslines that
stretched between the houses like a march of pale ghost
sheets. They did not meet one single person along the way,
another characteristic of this strangest of old cities: You
could walk for miles without seeing a soul, only cats and
rats on their hunt for prey in the garbage.

Before them the alley ended at the very edge of a canal.
There was no sidewalk along its banks, the walls of the

houses reached right down into the water. There wasn't a bridge to be seen.

"A dead end," Merle grumbled. "We have to go back again."

Serafin shook his head. "We're exactly where I wanted to be." He bent over the edge a bit and looked up at the sky. Then he looked across the water. "See that?"

Merle walked up next to him. Her eyes followed his index finger to the gently swelling surface. The brackish smell of the canal rose into her nose, but she hardly noticed it. Strands of algae were drifting about, far more than usual.

An illuminated window was reflected in the water, the only one far and wide. It was in the second floor of a house on the other side of the canal. The opposite bank was about fifty feet away.

"I don't know what you mean," she said.

"See the light in that window?"

"Sure."

Serafin pulled out a silver pocket watch, a valuable piece that probably came from his thieving days. He snapped open the lid. "Ten after twelve. We're on time."

"So?"

He grinned. "I'll explain. You see the reflection on the water, don't you?"

She nodded.

"Good. Now look at the house over it and show me the window that's reflected there. The one that's lit."

Merle looked up at the dark house front. All the windows were dark, not a single one lit. She looked down at the water again. The reflection remained unchanged: In one of the reflected windows a light was burning. When she looked up at the house again, that rectangle in the wall was dark.

"How can that be?" she asked, perplexed. "In the reflection the window is lit, but in reality it's pitch-black."

Serafin's grin got even wider. "Well, well."

"Magic?"

"Not entirely. Or maybe yes. Depending on how you look at it."

Her face darkened. "Couldn't you express yourself a little more clearly?"

"It happens in the hour after midnight. Between twelve and one at night the same phenomenon appears at several places in the city. Very few know about them, and even I don't know many of these places, but it's true: During this hour, a few houses cast a reflection on the water that doesn't tally with the reality. There are only tiny differences—lighted windows, sometimes another door, or people walking along in front of the houses while in reality there's nobody there."

"And what does it mean?"

"Nobody knows for sure. But there are rumors." He lowered his voice and acted very mysterious. "Stories about a *second* Venice."

"A second Venice?"

"One that only exists in the reflection in the water. Or at least lies so far away from us that it can't be reached, even with the fastest ship. Not even with the Empire's sunbarks. People say that it's in another world, which is so like ours and yet entirely different. And around midnight the border between the two cities becomes porous, perhaps just because it's so old and has gotten worn over the centuries, like a worn-out carpet."

Merle stared at him, her eyes wide. "You mean, that window with the light . . . you mean, it actually exists— only not *here*?"

"It gets even better. There was an old beggar who sat at this spot for years and watched day and night. He told me that sometimes men and women from this other Venice managed to cross the wall between the worlds. What they don't know, though, is that they're no longer human beings when they arrive here. They're only phantoms then, and they're caught forever in the mirrors of the city. Some of them manage to jump from mirror to mirror, and so every now and then they also stray into your master's workshop and into his magic mirrors."

Merle considered whether Serafin might perhaps be playing a joke on her. "You aren't just trying to put something over on me, are you?"

Serafin flashed a phony smile. "Do I really look as though I could swindle anyone?"

"Of course not, top-notch master thief."

"Believe me, I've actually heard this story. How much of it's the truth, I can't really say." He pointed to the illuminated window in the water. "However, some things support it."

"But that would mean that I was catching human beings in that glass ball the other day!"

"Don't worry about it. I've seen Arcimboldo throw them into the canal. They get out again somehow there."

"And now I understand what he meant when he said that the phantoms could settle into the reflections on the water." Merle gasped. "Arcimboldo knows! He knows the truth!"

"What are you going to do now? Ask him about it?"

She shrugged her shoulders. "Why not?" She didn't have a chance to pursue the thought further, for suddenly there was a movement on the water. As they looked down more attentively, a silhouette slid over the surface of the canal toward them.

"Is that—" She broke off as it became clear to her that the reflection was no illusion.

"Back!" Serafin had seen it at the same time.

They whipped into the alleyway and pressed tight against the wall.

From the left, something large glided over the water without touching it. It was a lion with mighty wings of feathers; like the entire body, they were also of stone.

Their tips almost touched the walls of the houses on both sides of the canal. The lion flew almost soundlessly, only its unhurried wingbeats producing subtle whishing like the drawing of breath. Their draft blew icily into Merle's and Serafin's faces. The enormous mass and weight of that body were deceptive; in the air it held itself as featherlight as a bird. Its front and back legs were bent, its mouth nearly closed. Behind its eyes sparkled a disconcerting shrewdness, far sharper than the understanding of ordinary animals.

A soldier sat grimly on the lion's back. His uniform was of black leather and trimmed with steel rivets. A bodyguard of the City Council, assigned to protect one of the big bosses personally. You didn't encounter them very often, and when you did, it usually meant nothing good.

The lion bearing its master floated past the opening of their alleyway without noticing the two of them. Merle and Serafin didn't dare breathe until the flying predator had left them far behind. Carefully they leaned forward and watched the lion gain altitude, leave the narrow canyon of the canal, and make a wide loop over the roofs of the district. Then it was lost to sight.

"He's circling," Serafin stated. "Whoever he's watching can't be far away."

"A councillor?" Merle whispered. "At this hour? In this district? Never in your life. They only leave their palaces when it's absolutely necessary."

"There aren't many lions that can fly. The few that are left never go any farther than necessary from their councillors." Serafin took a deep breath. "One of the councillors must be very close by."

As if to underline his words, the growl of a flying lion came out of the nighttime darkness. A second answered the call. Then a third.

"There are several." Merle shook her head in bafflement. "What are they doing here?"

Serafin's eyes gleamed. "We could find out."

"And the lions?"

"I've often run away from them before."

Merle wasn't sure if he was boasting or telling the truth. Perhaps both. She simply didn't know him well enough. Her instinct told her that she could trust him. *Must* trust him, it looked at the moment—for Serafin had already made his way to the other end of the alleyway.

She hurried after him until she came even with him again. "I hate having to run after other people."

"Sometimes it helps to get decisions made."

She snorted. "I hate it even more when other people want to make my decisions for me."

He stopped and held her back by the arm. "You're right. We both have to want this. It could get quite dangerous."

Merle sighed. "I'm not one of those girls who gives up easily—so don't treat me like one. And I'm not afraid of flying lions." *Of course not,* she said silently to herself, *I've never been chased by one either—yet.*

"No reason to be offended now."

"I'm not at all."

"You are so."

"And you keep picking a fight."

He grinned. "Occupational disease."

"Boaster! But you aren't a thief anymore." She left him standing and walked on. "Come on. Or there won't be lions or councillors or adventure tonight."

This time it was he who followed her. She had the feeling that he was testing her. Would she go in the same direction that he'd chosen? Would she interpret the distant wingbeats against the sky properly to lead them to their goal?

She'd show him where to go—literally, in fact.

She hurried around the next corner and kept looking up at the night sky between the edges of the roofs, until she finally slowed and took pains to make no more sound. From here on they ran the danger of being discovered. She just didn't know whether the danger threatened from the sky or from one of the doorways.

"It's that house over there," Serafin whispered.

Her eye followed his index finger to the entrance of a narrow building, just wide enough for a door and two boarded-up windows. It seemed to have once been a servants' annex to one of the neighboring grand houses, in

117

days when the facades of Venice still bore witness to wealth and magnificence. But today many of the palazzi stood just as empty as the houses on the Canal of the Expelled and elsewhere. Not even tramps and beggars squatted there, for in winter the gigantic rooms were impossible to heat. Firewood had been a scarce commodity since the beginning of the siege, and so the stripping of the abandoned buildings of the city had begun long ago, breaking out their wooden floors and beams in order to heat the woodstoves in the cold months.

"How do you know it's this particular house?" Merle asked softly.

Serafin gestured to the roof. Merle had to admit that he had astonishingly good eyes: Something peeked over the edge of the roof, a stone paw, which scratched the tiles. It was impossible to see the lions from the street. Nevertheless, Merle did not doubt that watchful eyes were staring down out of the darkness.

"Let's try around back," Serafin suggested softly.

"But the back side of the house is right on the canal!" Merle's sense of direction in the narrow alleyways was unbeatable. She knew exactly how it looked behind this row of houses. The walls there were smooth, and there was no walk along the edge of the canal.

"We'll manage anyhow," said Serafin. "Trust me."

"As friend or master thief?"

He stopped for a moment, tilted his head, and looked

at her in amazement. Then he stuck out his hand. "Friends?" he asked carefully.

She took his hand firmly in her own. "Friends."

Serafin beamed. "Then I say to you as master thief that somehow we are going to get inside this house. And as friend—" He hesitated, then went on, "as friend I promise you that I will never let you down, no matter what happens tonight."

He didn't wait for her reply but pulled her with him, back into the shadows of the alleyway out of which they had come. Unerringly they made their way through tunnels, across a back courtyard, and through empty houses.

It seemed almost no time until they were edging their way along a narrow ledge that ran along the back of a row of buildings. The pitch-dark water rocked below them. About twenty yards farther, vague in the faint moonlight, the curved outline of a bridge was discernible. And at its highest point stood a lion with an armed rider. If he were to turn around, he would surely be able to spot them in the darkness.

"I hope the lion doesn't sense us," Merle whispered. Like Serafin, she was pressing herself flat against the wall. The ledge was just wide enough for her heels. She had trouble trying to keep her balance and at the same time keep her eye on the sentry on the bridge.

Serafin had less difficulty negotiating the ledge. He was accustomed to getting into strange houses in the most unusual ways, first as a thief, then as Umberto's secret courier. Still, he didn't give Merle the feeling she was holding him back.

"Why doesn't he turn around?" he burst out through clenched teeth. "I don't like that."

Since Merle was a little smaller than he was, she could see a little farther under the bridge. Now she saw that a boat was approaching from the opposite direction. She reported her discovery to Serafin in a whisper. "The guard doesn't seem bothered by it. It looks as though he's been waiting for the boat."

"A secret meeting," Serafin guessed. "I've seen those a few times—a councillor meeting one of his informants. They say the councillors have spies everywhere, in all sorts of people."

Merle had other concerns at the moment. "How much farther is it?"

Serafin bent over a fraction of an inch. "About ten feet, then we're at the first window. If it's open, we can climb into the house." He looked around at Merle. "Can you tell who's in the boat?"

She blinked hard, hoping to be able to see the figure in the bow more clearly. But, like both the oarsmen sitting farther behind him, he was wrapped in a dark hooded cloak. No wonder, considering the time and the cold, and yet Merle shivered at the look of him. Was she mistaken, or did the lion on the bridge paw the ground nervously?

Serafin reached the window. Now they were no more than ten yards away from the bridge. He looked carefully through the glass and nodded to Merle. "The room's empty. They must be waiting somewhere else in the house."

"Can you get the window open?" Merle wasn't really subject to dizziness, but her back had begun to hurt and a tingling was creeping up her outspread legs.

Serafin pressed against the glass, first gently, then a little harder. A slight crack sounded. The right window swung inward on its hinges.

Merle sighed in relief. Thank goodness! She tried to keep her eye on the boat while Serafin climbed into the house. The dinghy had tied up on the other side of the bridge. The lion bore its rider to firm ground to receive the hooded and mantled figure.

Merle saw flying lions in the sky. At least three, perhaps more. If one of them should swoop down again and fly along the canal, it would discover her immediately.

But then Serafin reached his hand to her through the window and pulled her inside the house. She gasped as she felt wooden planks under her feet. She could have kissed the floor with relief. Or Serafin. Better not. She felt her cheeks flush red.

"Are you all right?" he asked.

"I was working hard," she replied quickly and turned away. "What next?"

He took his time answering. At first she thought he was still staring at her; then she realized that he was listening, quite like the way Junipa had listened during their journey along the Canal of the Expelled—highly concentrated, so that not the slightest sound escaped him.

"They're farther front in the house," he said at last. "At least two men, possibly even three."

"With the soldiers that makes it roughly half a dozen."

"Afraid?"

"Not a bit."

He smiled. "*Who's* the boaster here?"

She couldn't help returning his smile. He could see through her, even in the dark. With anyone else that would have made her uncomfortable. "Trust me," he'd said, and in fact, she did trust him. Everything had gone much too fast, but she had no time to worry about it.

Quiet as mice, they slipped out of the room and felt their way down a pitch-black hallway. At its end lay the front door. A shimmer of candlelight was falling through the first corridor on the right. On their left a flight of stairs led up to the second floor.

Serafin brought his lips very close to Merle's ear. "Wait here. I'm going to look around."

She wanted to protest, but he quickly shook his head.

"Please," he added.

With heavy heart she looked after him as he quickly tiptoed to the lighted hallway. At any moment the front door could open and the man in the hooded cape come in, accompanied by the soldiers.

Serafin reached the doorway, looked carefully through it, waited a moment, then turned back to Merle. Silently he pointed to the stairs to the upper floor.

She followed his instruction noiselessly. He was the master thief, not she. Perhaps he knew best what to do, even if it was hard for her to admit it. She was usually unwilling to do what others told her to—whether or not it was in her own best interest.

The stairs were of solid stone. Merle went up and on the second floor made her way to the room that lay over the candlelit room on the ground floor. There she understood what had drawn Serafin upstairs.

A third of the floor had fallen in a long time ago. Wooden beams were scattered and splintered away from the edges, framing a wide opening in the center of the room. From below, candles sent a faint light. Low voices could be heard. Their tone sounded uncertain and apprehensive, even though Merle couldn't make out the exact words.

"Three men," Serafin whispered in her ear. "All three city councillors. Big bosses."

Merle peeked over the edge. She felt the warmth of the light rising to her face. Serafin was right. The three men standing next to one another down there in the light of the candles wore the long robes of Council members, golden and purple and scarlet.

In all of Venice there was no higher authority than the City Council. Since the invasion by the Empire and the loss of all contact with the mainland, they had jurisdiction over the affairs of the besieged city. They had all powers in their hands and they maintained the connection with the Flowing Queen—at least that's what they said. They posed to the public as men of the world and infallible. But among the people, there were guarded whispers of misuse of power, nepotism, and the decadence of the old noble families, to which most of the city councillors belonged. It was no secret that those who had money received preference, and anyone who bore an old family name counted more than ordinary folk.

One of the three men on the ground floor was holding a small wooden box in his hands. It looked like a jewel casket made of ebony.

"What're they doing here?" Merle mouthed silently.

Serafin shrugged his shoulders.

There was a grating sound down below. The front door was opened. There were footsteps, then the voice of a soldier.

"My lords councillor," he announced respectfully, "the Egyptian envoy has arrived."

"For heaven's sake, shut your mouth!" hissed the councillor in the purple robe. "Or do you want the entire district to hear of it?"

The soldier withdrew and left the house, and his

companion entered the room. It was the man from the boat, and even now he wore his hood drawn deep over his face. The candlelight wasn't enough to illuminate the shadows under it.

He dispensed with a greeting. "You have carried out what you promised?"

Merle had never heard an Egyptian speak. She was surprised that the man's words showed no accent. But she was too tense to evaluate the significance of the situation right away. Only gradually did its enormous import sink in: a secret meeting between City Council members and an envoy of the Egyptians! A spy, probably, who lived in the city undercover, or otherwise his Venetian dialect wouldn't have been so perfect.

Serafin was chalk white. Drops of sweat beaded his forehead. In shock he peered over the edge into the room below.

The councillor in gold bowed respectfully and the two others did the same after him. "We are glad that you have agreed to this meeting. And certainly, we have carried out what you requested."

The councillor in scarlet nervously clasped his fingers. "The Pharaoh will show himself grateful, won't he?"

With a jerk, the black opening of the hood turned toward him. "God-Emperor Amenophis will learn of your request to join with us. What happens then lies in his divine hands alone."

"Certainly, certainly," the purple councillor hastened to appease him. He cast an angry look toward the man in the scarlet robe. "We do not intend to question any decision of His Divinity."

"Where is it?"

The councillor in gold held the jewel casket out to the envoy. "With most humble greetings to Pharaoh Amenophis. From his loyal servants."

Traitor, thought Merle in utter contempt. *Traitor, traitor, traitor!* It made her really sick to hear the groveling tone of the three city councillors. Or was it just the fear that was turning her stomach?

The envoy took the jewel casket and opened the catch. The councillors exchanged uneasy looks.

Merle bent over farther to better see the contents of the box. Serafin, too, tried to see exactly what was in there.

The casket was lined with velvet, on which lay a little vial of crystal, no longer than a finger. The envoy carefully lifted it out, heedlessly letting the casket fall. It crashed on the floor with a bang. As one, the councillors jumped at the sound.

Between thumb and forefinger the man held the vial up to the opening of his hood, directly against the light of the candles.

"Finally, after all these years!" he murmured absently.

Merle looked at Serafin in amazement. What was so valuable in such a tiny vial?

The councillor in purple raised his hands in a solemn gesture. "It is she, truly. The essence of the Flowing Queen. The charm you placed at our disposal has worked a true wonder."

Merle held her breath and exchanged alarmed looks with Serafin.

"The Pharaoh's alchemists have worked on it for twice ten years," said the envoy coolly. "There was never any doubt that the charm would be effective."

"Of course not, of course not."

The councillor in scarlet, who'd already made himself unpleasantly conspicuous, was rocking excitedly from one foot to the other. "But all your magic wouldn't have helped you if we hadn't declared ourselves ready to perform it in the presence of the Flowing Queen. A servant of the Pharaoh would never have gotten so near her."

The envoy's tone turned wary. "So, are you then *not* a servant of the Pharaoh, Councillor de Angeliis?"

The other's face went white. "Certainly I am, certainly, certainly."

"You are nothing but a whining coward. And of those the worst kind: a traitor!"

The councillor wrinkled his nose defiantly. He shook off the hand that the councillor in purple tried to place soothingly on his arm. "Without us you'd never—"

"Councillor de Angeliis!" scolded the envoy, and now he sounded like an angry old woman. "You will receive recompense for your service of friendship, if that is your concern. At the latest when the Pharaoh makes his entrance into the lagoon with his armies and confirms you as his representative in office. But now, in Amenophis's name, will you be quiet!"

"With your permission," said the councillor in purple, paying no attention to the wretched-looking de Angeliis. "You should know that time is pressing. Recently a messenger from Hell has arrived to offer us a pact against the Empire. I don't know how long we can continue to resist that. Others on the City Council are more receptive to this messenger than we are. It won't be possible to hold them in check indefinitely. Especially as the messenger has said that next time he'll appear in public so that *all* the people will learn of his demands."

The envoy expelled his breath in a wheeze. "That must not happen. The attack on the lagoon is imminent. A pact with Hell can bring it all to nothing." He was silent a moment as he considered the situation. "If the messenger actually appears, make sure that he can't get to the people. Kill him."

"And the vengeance of Hell—," de Angeliis began in a subdued voice, but the third councillor motioned him to silence with a wave.

"Certainly, sir," said the councillor in gold, with a bow in the direction of the envoy. "As you command. The Empire will protect us from all consequences when it once has the city under its control."

The Egyptian nodded graciously. "So shall it be."

Merle's lungs desperately demanded air—she couldn't hold her breath one second longer. The sound was soft, barely audible, but still loud enough to alert the councillor in scarlet. He looked up at the hole in the ceiling. Merle and Serafin pulled their heads back just in time. So they only heard the envoy's further words but couldn't see what was going on.

"The desert crystal of the vial is strong enough to hold the Flowing Queen. Her regency over the lagoon is ended. An army of many thousands of soldiers stands ready on land and on the water. As soon as the Pharaoh holds this vial in his hands, the galleys and sunbarks will strike."

Merle felt a movement at her right side. She looked around, but Serafin was too far away. However, something was moving at her hip! A rat? The truth first hit her when it was already too late.

The water mirror slid out of her dress pocket like something alive, with jerky, clumsy movements like a blinded animal. Then everything went at breakneck speed. Merle tried to grab the mirror, but it shot underneath her hand, skidded to the edge of the hole in the floor, slipped out over it—and fell.

In a long moment, as if frozen in time, Merle saw that the surface of the mirror had become milky, fogged by the presence of the phantom.

The mirror plunged past Merle's outstretched hand

into the depths. It fell exactly on the envoy, missed his hood, struck his hand, and knocked the crystal vial out of his fingers. The man howled, with pain, with rage, with surprise, as the mirror and the vial landed on the floor almost at the same time.

"No!" Serafin's cry made the three councillors leap away from each other like drops of hot fat. With a daring bound he swung himself over the edge and sprang into the middle of them. Merle had no time to consider this sudden chain of catastrophes. She followed Serafin over the edge, her dress fluttering around her, and with a loud bellow that was intended to sound grim but was probably anything but.

The envoy avoided her. Otherwise her feet would have hit his head. Hastily he bent and tried to pick up the vial. But his fingers reached past the vial and brushed across the water mirror. For a fraction of a second his fingertips furrowed the surface, vanished under it—and were gone when the envoy pulled back his hand with a scream of pain. Instead of fingertips there were black slivers of bone, which stuck out of the remainders of his fingers, smoking and burned, as if he'd stuck his hand in a beaker of acid.

A mad shrieking came from under the hood. The sound was inhuman because no face appeared to give it; the screaming poured from an invisible mouth.

Serafin did a cartwheel on both hands, almost too fast for the eye to see. When he came to a stop by the window, he held the vial in his right hand and Merle's mirror in his left.

Meanwhile the councillor in purple, the traitors' spokesman, had grabbed Merle by the upper arm and tried to pull her around. With balled fist he raised his arm to strike her, while the two other councillors ran around like frightened hens, bellowing loudly for their bodyguards. Merle dodged him and was able to shake his hand off her arm, but as she did so her back thumped against black stuff. The robe of the envoy. There was a stench of burned flesh around him.

A sharp draft whistled through the cracks of the boarded-up windows: Flying lions had landed outside in front of the house. Steel scraped over steel as sabers were withdrawn from their sheaths.

Someone placed an arm around Merle from behind, but she ducked away under it as she had in so many scraps in the orphanage. She'd had practice in fighting, and she knew what she had to hit so that it hurt. When Councillor de Angeliis put himself in her way, she placed a well-aimed kick. The fat man in the scarlet robe bellowed as if he'd been spitted, holding his lower abdomen with both hands.

"Out!" cried Serafin, holding the two other councillors in check by threatening to smash the vial on the floor—whatever that might bring about.

Merle raced over to him and ran at his side to the exit.

They turned into the corridor at the very moment the front door burst open and two bodyguards in black leather thundered in.

"By the Ancient Traitor!" Serafin cursed.

Nonplussed, the soldiers stopped in their tracks. They had been expecting a trick by the Egyptian, with men armed to the teeth, worthy opponents for two battle-hardened heroes of the Guard. Instead they saw a girl in a ragged dress and a boy who held in his hands two gleaming objects that looked not at all like knives.

Merle and Serafin used the moment of surprise. Before the guards could react, the two were on their way to the back room.

There, in front of the open window, the envoy was waiting for them. He had known that there was only one way of escape. At the back, out to the water.

"The mirror!" Merle called to Serafin.

He threw it over to her, and she caught it with both hands, grabbed it by the handle, and hit at the envoy with it. He avoided it skillfully, but that also left the way to the window free. His singed fingertips still smoked.

"The vial!" he demanded in a hissing voice. "You are setting yourselves against the Pharaoh!"

Serafin let out a daredevil laugh that surprised even Merle. Then he somersaulted past the envoy, between his outstretched hands. He landed safely on the windowsill and sat there like a bird, with both feet on the frame, knees drawn up, and a wide grin on his lips.

"All honor to the Flowing Queen!" he cried out, while Merle used the moment to spring to his side. "Follow me!"

With that he let himself fall backward out the window into the waters of the still canal.

It wasn't really his hand that drew Merle after him: It was his enthusiasm, his sheer will not to give up. For the first time in her life she felt admiration for another person.

The envoy screeched and grabbed the edge of Merle's dress, but it was with the fingers of his eroded hand, and he let go again with a yelp of pain.

The water was icy. In a single heartbeat it seemed to pierce her clothes, her flesh, her entire body. Merle could no longer breathe, nor move, nor even think. She didn't know how long this condition lasted—it seemed to her like minutes—but when she surfaced, Serafin was beside her, and life came back to her limbs. She couldn't have been under for more than a few seconds.

"Here, take this!" Underwater he pressed the vial into her left hand. In the right she was still holding the mirror, which lay between her fingers as if it grew there.

"What shall I do with it?"

"If worse comes to worst, I'll steer them away," said Serafin and spat water. The waves slapped at his lips.

Worse comes to worst, Merle thought. Even worse?

The envoy appeared in the window and shouted something.

Serafin let out a whistle. It only worked on the second try; the first just spewed water from his lips. Merle followed his eyes to the window, then saw black silhouettes slip down, four-legged shadows that sprang from holes and drainpipes, screeching and meowing, with unsheathed claws, which they sank into the robe of the envoy. One cat came up on the windowsill, immediately launched again, and disappeared completely into the dark of the hood. Screaming, the Egyptian staggered backward into the room.

"Harmless thieves' trick!" observed Serafin with satisfaction.

"We have to get out of the water!" Merle turned and let the mirror slide into the pocket of her dress, together with the vial, to which she gave no further thought for the moment. She swam a few strokes in the direction of the opposite bank. The walls came down to the canal there, and there was no hold for pulling oneself to dry land. All the same, she had to do something!

"Onto land?" Serafin said, looking up at the sky. "It looks as though that's going to take care of itself."

Breathlessly Merle turned around, much too slowly, because her dress hindered her in the water. And then she saw what he meant.

Two lions, wings outspread, were diving steeply down at them out of the black of the night.

"Duck!" she screamed and didn't see whether Serafin followed her command. She held her breath and glided underwater, felt the salty cold on her lips, the pressure in her ears and nose. The canal must be about nine feet deep, and she knew that she needed to get at least half of that between her and the lions' claws.

She saw and heard nothing of what was happening around her. When she was deep enough, she turned herself horizontal, and plunged along the canal with a few strong strokes. Perhaps she could make it if she could reach one of the old loading doors.

At one time, when Venice had been an important trading city, the merchants had been able to bring their wares into their houses from the canals through doors that lay at surface level. Today many of these houses stood empty, their owners long dead, but the doors still existed, usually rotten, eaten away by water and by salt. Often the bottom third was rotted away. For Merle they offered an ideal chance for escape.

And Serafin?

She could only pray that he was behind her, not too far above, where the lions' claws could grab him out of the water. Stone lions are shy of water, have always been, and the last flying examples of their kind are no exception. They may put their claws into the water, but they themselves will never, ever dip into it. Merle knew this weakness of the lions and she hoped with all her might that Serafin did too.

Gradually she grew starved for air and in her need she sent a fervent prayer to the Flowing Queen. Then it occurred to her that the Flowing Queen was in a vial in the pocket of her dress, imprisoned like a genie in a bottle and probably as helpless as she was.

The essence of the Flowing Queen, the councillor had said.

Where was Serafin? And where was there a door?

She was losing consciousness. The black around her seemed to turn, and she felt as if she were falling deeper and deeper, while in truth she was struggling toward the top, to reach the surface.

Then she broke through. Air flowed into her lungs. She opened her eyes.

She had come farther than she'd hoped. Very close by there was in fact a door, slanting and ragged, where the water had licked at the wood over and over and finally rotted it. The upper half hung undamaged on its hinges, but under it gaped a dark maw into the interior of the house. The rotted wood looked like the jaw of a sea monster, a row of sharp teeth, cracked and green with algae and mold.

"Merle!"

Serafin's voice made her whirl around in the water. What she saw numbed her from head to toe. She almost went under.

One of the lions was hovering over the water and

holding the kicking Serafin in its front paws, like a fish that it had grabbed and plucked out of the stream.

"Merle!" Serafin bellowed once more. She knew now that he hadn't seen her at all, that he didn't know where she was and if she were still alive. He was afraid for her. He feared she had drowned.

Her mind screamed to answer him, to draw the notice of the lions to herself in order to give him a chance to get away. But she was only fooling herself. No lion lets go of what it has caught.

Already the beast completed a turn with a well-aimed wingbeat, moved away, and rose in the air, the defenseless Serafin firmly pressed under its body.

"Merle, wherever you are," bellowed Serafin in a voice growing fainter, "you must flee! Hide yourself! Save the Flowing Queen!"

Then lion, rider, and Serafin vanished into the night like a cloud of ash dispersed on the wind.

Merle ducked under again. Her tears became one with the canal, became one with it as did Merle herself. On and on, as she dove through the wooden, toothed maw, through the rotted door into still deeper darkness; as she pulled herself to dryness in the dark, curled up like a little child, simply lay there, and wept.

Breathed and wept.

6
END AND BEGINNING

THE FLOWING QUEEN WAS SPEAKING TO HER.

"*Merle,*" said her voice. "*Merle, listen to me!*"

Merle started up, her eyes quickly searching the darkness. The old storeroom reeked of dampness and rotten wood. The only light came in through the broken door from the canal. There was a shimmer and shining in the air—someone was searching the water surface with torches out there!

She had to get out of here as quickly as possible.

"*You are not dreaming, Merle.*"

The words were in her; the voice was speaking between her ears.

"Who are you?" she whispered, leaping to her feet.

"You know who I am. Do not be afraid of me."

Merle pulled the mirror out of her pocket and held it in the flickering torchlight. The surface was clear, the phantom nowhere to be seen. But she also felt that it wasn't he who was speaking to her. She quickly slid the mirror back into her pocket and took out the vial. It fit comfortably into her hand.

"You?" If she only spoke in single words, not in entire sentences, maybe it wouldn't be apparent how very much her voice quavered.

"You must get away from here. They are going to search through all the houses that border on the canal. And after that, the rest of the district."

"What's happened to Serafin?"

"He is now a prisoner of the Guard."

"They'll kill him!"

"Perhaps. But not right away. They could have done that already, in the water. They are going to try to find out who you are and where they can find you."

Merle shoved the vial back into her pocket and felt her way through the darkness. She was miserably cold in her wet dress, but her goose pimples had nothing to do with the temperature.

"Are you the Flowing Queen?" she asked softly.

"Do you want to call me that? Queen?"

"First of all I just want to get away from here."

"Then we should attend to that."

"We? I see only one person here who has legs to run away with."

In the dark she found a door that led back into the house. She slipped through it and found herself in a deserted entry hall. Floor and banisters were covered with thick dust. Merle's feet left tracks in the dust as if it were a blanket of snow. Her pursuers wouldn't find it hard to follow her trail.

The front door was nailed shut from the outside, like many doors in Venice these days, but she found a window whose glass she was able to break with the fallen head of a statue. By some miracle she climbed out without cutting either hands or knees.

What now? Best go back to the Canal of the Expelled. Arcimboldo would know what to do. Or Eft. Or Junipa. Someone or other! She couldn't carry this secret around with her alone.

"If your friend talks, they will look for you there first," warned the voice suddenly.

"Serafin will never betray me!" she retorted, annoyed. And in her thoughts she added: *He swore never to let me down.*

On the other hand, she had watched passively as the lion carried him away. But what could she have done anyway?

"Nothing," said the voice. *"You were helpless. You are still."*

"Are you reading my thoughts?"

She got no answer to that, which was answer enough.

"Stop that," she said sharply. "I saved you. You owe me something."

Further silence. Had she angered the voice? So much the better; maybe it would leave her in peace then. It was hard enough to think for one person alone. She needed no inner voice, questioning her every decision.

Cautiously she ran down the alleyway, stopping again and again, listening for pursuers and suspicious sounds. She even kept her eye on the sky, although it was dark enough that a whole pride of lions could have been romping around high up there. It was still hours till sunrise.

Soon she knew where she was: only a few corners away from Campo San Polo. She'd covered half the distance back to the workshop. Not much farther and she would be safe.

"*Not safe,*" contradicted the voice. "*Not as long as the boy is a prisoner.*"

Merle exploded. "What is this?" she shouted, her voice resounding loudly from the walls. "What are you? My voice of reason?"

"*I will be that, if you want.*"

"I only want you to leave me in peace."

"*I am only giving you advice, not orders.*"

"I don't need advice."

"*But I am afraid you do need it.*"

Merle stopped, looked angrily around, and found a gap in a boarded-up wall between two houses. She had to settle this business once and for all, here and now. She squeezed herself through the opening, drew deeper back into the dark canyon between the house walls, and sank down with her knees drawn up.

"You want to talk with me? Well, then, we'll talk."

"*As you wish.*"

"Who or what are you?"

"*I think you already know that.*"

"The Flowing Queen?"

"*At the moment, only a voice in your head.*"

Merle hesitated. If the voice really belonged to the Queen, wouldn't it then be polite to deal with her a little more respectfully? But she was still full of doubt. "You don't talk like a queen."

"*I talk like you. I speak with your voice, with your thoughts.*"

"I'm only some girl."

"*Now you are more than that. You have undertaken a task.*"

"I have undertaken nothing at all!" Merle said. "I didn't want all this. And don't talk to me now about fate and such nonsense. This isn't a fairy tale."

"*Unfortunately, it is not. In a fairy tale, matters are simpler. You go home and find that the soldiers have* burned down your house and carried off your friends, you become angry, recognize that you must take up the battle against the Pharaoh, meet him finally, and kill him through a trick. That would be the fairy tale. But unfortunately we have to deal with the reality. The path is the same one and yet different."

"I could simply take the vial and tip whatever's in it into the nearest canal."

"No! That would kill me!"

"Then you aren't the Flowing Queen. She's at home in the canal."

"The Flowing Queen is only what you wish her to be. At the moment, a fluid in a vial. And a voice in your head."

"That's confused nonsense. I don't understand you."

"The Egyptians drove me out of the canal by laying a spell on the water. That is the only reason the traitors succeeded in imprisoning me in this vial. The magic still permeates the water of the lagoon, and it will last for months before it has evaporated. Until then my essence cannot be combined with the water."

"We all thought that you were something . . . something different."

"Sorry to disappoint you."

"Something spiritual."

"Like God?"

"Yes, I guess so."

"*Even God is only always in those who believe in him. Just as I am in you now.*"

"That's not the same. You left me no choice. You talked to me. I must believe in you, otherwise . . ."

"*Otherwise what?*"

"Otherwise it would mean that I'm crazy. That I'm only talking to myself."

"*Would that be so bad, then? To listen to the voice inside you?*"

Merle shook her head impatiently. "That's hair-splitting. You're only trying to confuse me. Perhaps you really are only that dumb phantom who went into my mirror."

"*Put me to the test. Leave the mirror lying somewhere. Separate from it. Then you will see that I am still with you.*"

"I will never give up the mirror voluntarily. I treasure it, as you know very well."

"*It is not going to be forever. Only for a moment. Put it down at the end of this little alley, come back here, and listen to see if I am still there.*"

Merle thought it over briefly, then agreed. She carried the mirror to the farthest corner of the alleyway, about fifteen yards from the entrance. She had to step over all sorts of trash that had collected there over the years. She drove away rats with her feet, and they snapped at her heels. Finally, leaving the mirror, she ran back to the front end of the alleyway.

"Well?" she asked softly.

"Here I am," responded the voice with amusement.

Merle sighed. "Does that mean you continue to claim that you're the Flowing Queen?"

"I never claimed that. You said it."

Merle hurried back to the mirror and picked it up. Quickly she dropped it into her dress pocket and buttoned the pocket closed. "You said you used my words and my thoughts. Does that also mean that you can influence my will?"

"Even if I could, I would not do it."

"I guess I have to believe you, huh?"

"Trust me."

It was the second time tonight that someone had asked that of her. She didn't like it at all.

"Nevertheless, it could be that I am only imagining all this, couldn't it?"

"Which would you prefer? An imaginary voice that speaks to you or a real one?"

"Neither one."

"I will enlist your services no longer than necessary."

Merle opened her eyes wide. "My *services?*"

"I need your help. The Egyptian spy and the traitors will stop at nothing to get me into their power. They will hunt you. We must leave Venice."

"Leave the city? But that's impossible! There's been a siege for more than thirty years, and they say it's just as tight as on the first day."

The voice sounded stricken. *"I have given my best, but at last I also have fallen victim to the enemy's tricks. I can no longer protect the lagoon. We must find another way."*

"But . . . but what about all the people? And the mermaids?"

"No one can keep the Egyptians from invading. At the moment they are still not certain what has happened to me. That helps us with a delay. But there is only a little time left before they find out the truth. And the city is only safe until they do."

"That's nothing but a temporary reprieve."

"Yes," said the voice sadly. *"Nothing more and nothing less. But when the Pharaoh's fist closes around the lagoon, he will be looking for you. The envoy knows your face. He will not rest until you are dead."*

Merle thought about Junipa and Serafin, about Arcimboldo and Eft. About all those who meant something to her. She should just leave these people behind and flee?

"Not flee," contradicted the voice. *"But go on the quest. I will never give it up. If it dies, I die as well. But we must leave the city to find help."*

"There's no one left outside anymore to help us. The Empire has ruled over the whole world for a long time."

"Perhaps. Perhaps not, too."

Merle had had enough of these enigmatic hintings, even though she was gradually losing any doubt that the

146

voice in her head actually belonged to the Flowing Queen. And although she'd grown up in a city in which the Queen was venerated exceedingly, she wanted to show no reverence. She hadn't asked to be drawn into this mess.

"First I'm going back to the workshop," said Merle. "I have to speak with Junipa, and with Arcimboldo.

"We will lose valuable time."

"That's my decision!" Merle retorted angrily.

"As you will."

"Does that mean you aren't going to try to talk me out of it?"

"Yes."

That surprised her, but it gave her back a little of her self-confidence.

She was just about to climb out of the space between the boards to the alley when the voice spoke again.

"There is still one thing."

"And?"

"I cannot remain much longer in this vial."

"Why not?"

"The desert crystal numbs my brain."

Merle smiled. "Does that mean you'll talk less?"

"It means that I will die. My essence must bind with living organisms. The water of the lagoon is full of them. But the vial is only cold, dead crystal. I am going to wither like a plant that is withdrawn from the soil and the light."

"How can I help you?"

"*You must drink me.*"

Merle made a face. "Drink . . . you?"

"*We must become one, you and I.*"

"You're already in my head. And now you want my entire body, too? Do you know the saying about someone to whom you give your little finger and instead he takes the whole—"

"*I will die, Merle. And the lagoon with me.*"

"That's blackmail, you know that? If I don't help you, everyone will die. If I don't drink you, everyone will die. What comes next?"

"*Drink me, Merle.*"

She pulled the vial out of her pocket. The facets of the crystal sparkled like an insect's eye. "And there's no other way?"

"*None.*"

"How will you . . . I mean, how will you get out of me again, and when?"

"*When the time for it has come.*"

"I thought you'd say something like that."

"*I would not ask you to do it if we had a choice.*"

Merle thought for a brief moment about the fact that she very much did have a choice. She could still throw away the vial and act as if this night had never taken place. But how could she lie to herself about all that had happened? Serafin, the fight with the envoy, the Flowing Queen.

Sometimes responsibility sneaked up on you without your seeing it coming, and then, very suddenly, it wouldn't let you go anymore.

Merle pulled out the stopper of the vial and sniffed at it. Nothing, no smell.

"How . . . umm, how do you taste, actually?"

"Like anything you want."

"How about fresh raspberries?"

"Why not?"

After a final hesitation, Merle put the opening to her mouth and drank. The fluid inside it was clear and cool, like water. Two, three swallows, no more, and then the vial was empty.

"That didn't taste like raspberries!"

"What, then?"

"Nothing at all."

"Then it was not as bad as you thought, was it?"

"I can't stand it when people trick me."

"It will not happen again. Do you feel any different now?"

Merle listened within, but she could find no change. The contents of the vial might just as well have been water.

"Same as before."

"Good. Then throw away the empty vial now. They must not find it on you."

Merle put the stopper back in the little crystal vial and shoved it under a heap of garbage. Gradually she realized what had just happened.

"Do I really now carry the Flowing Queen inside me?"

"*You always have. Like anyone who believes in her.*"

"That sounds like churches and priests and religious twaddle."

The voice in her head sighed. "*If it reassures you: I am now in you. Really in you.*"

Merle frowned, then shrugged. "Guess it's too late to change it."

The voice was quiet. Merle took that for reason to finally leave her hiding place. As quickly as she could she ran through the alleys to the Canal of the Expelled. She kept close to the walls of the houses so that she couldn't be seen from the sky. Perhaps the heavens were now swarming with the lions of the Guard.

"*I do not think so,*" countered the Flowing Queen. "*There are only three city councillors who betrayed me, and they have to be content with their share of the bodyguards. No councillor commands more than two flying lions. That makes six altogether, at the most.*"

"Six lions with nothing else to do but hunt me?" Merle exclaimed. "And that's supposed to reassure me? Thanks very much!"

"*Don't mention it.*"

"You don't know much about us humans, right?"

"*I have never had the opportunity to find out more about you.*"

Merle shook her head dumbly. For centuries now the

Flowing Queen had been honored, there were cults dedicated entirely to worshipping her. But the Queen herself knew nothing of it. Knew nothing about humans, nothing about what she meant to them.

She was the lagoon. But was she also therefore a god?

"Is the Pharaoh a god because the Egyptians honor him as a god?" asked the voice. *"For them he may be one. For you not. Divinity is only in the eye of the beholder."*

Merle was not in the mood to think about that, so instead she asked, "Before, that business with the mirror, that was you, wasn't it?"

"No."

"Then was it the mirror itself? Or the phantom in it?"

"Have you considered that you yourself could have thrown it at the envoy?"

"I would certainly have known about that."

"You are listening to a voice in your head that is perhaps only your own. It is possible that you also do things without being conscious of them—only because they are right."

"Nonsense."

"As you will."

She wasted no more words on it, but the thought wouldn't let go of Merle. What if she really was only imagining the voice of the Flowing Queen? What if she had been talking the whole time with a hallucination? And worse yet, what if her own actions were no longer under her control and she was talking with supernatural powers that in truth didn't exist at all?

This idea frightened her more than the fact that something strange had established itself in her. On the other hand, she didn't feel this stranger at all. It was all so terribly confusing.

Merle reached the mouth of the Canal of the Expelled. The festival hadn't ended yet—a few stalwarts sat on the bridge talking softly or staring silently into their cups. Junipa and the boys were nowhere to be seen. Probably they'd made their way home long since.

Merle ran along the small path at the edge of the canal until she reached Arcimboldo's workshop. The water lapped, whispering, against the stone. One last time she looked up at the night sky and imagined the lions were up there circling, beyond the shine of all the gaslights and torches. The soldiers on their backs might be blind in the dark, but weren't cats nocturnal animals? In her mind she saw the yellow predator eyes, which stared full of bloodlust into the depths, on the lookout for a girl in wet, worn clothes, with stringy hair and knowledge that might mean death.

She knocked on the door. No one answered. She pounded again. The blows sounded louder than usual to her; they must be audible throughout the whole district. Perhaps a lion was already on the way here, just now diving straight down through the layers of cold air, then through the smog over the city, the smoke of fires and chimneys, the weak shine of the lanterns, straight at Merle. She looked up in alarm, above her in the dark, and perhaps there actually was something there, gigantic wings of stone, paws as large as puppies and—

The door opened. Eft grabbed her by the arm and pulled her into the house. "Whatever were you thinking of to just run away?" The mermaid's eyes were glowing with anger as she slammed the front door behind Merle. "I had really expected more sense from you than—"

"I must speak with the master." Merle looked anxiously back at the door.

"*There was no one there,*" said the Queen reassuringly.

"With the master?" asked Eft. Obviously she couldn't hear the voice. "Have you any idea how late it is?"

"I'm sorry. Really. But it's important."

She held Eft's gaze and tried to read the mermaid's eyes. You are touched by the Flowing Queen, she had said to her. In hindsight the words sounded almost like a prophecy that had been fulfilled this night. Could Eft feel the change that had taken place in Merle? Did she sense the strange presence in her thoughts?

Whatever reason she might have, she stopped scolding Merle. Instead she turned around. "Come along."

Silently they went to the door of the workshop. Eft left Merle standing there. "Arcimboldo is still at work. He works every night. Tell him what you have to tell." With that she disappeared into the darkness and soon Merle could no longer hear her steps.

Alone, she hesitated before the door. It cost her great effort to raise her hand and knock. What could she say to Arcimboldo? Really the whole truth? Wouldn't he say she was crazy and throw her out of the house? And even worse: Mustn't she make clear to him at once what a threat she presented to the workshop and its inhabitants?

Nevertheless she felt a remarkable certainty that it was right to speak with him about it instead of with Eft. The mermaid worshipped the Flowing Queen. Merle's story would sound like blasphemy to her ears, the talk of a girl who wanted to make herself important.

Steps sounded on the other side of the door, then Arcimboldo's face appeared in the crack. "Merle! You're back!"

She hadn't expected him to have been aware of her disappearance at all. Eft must have told him of it.

"Come in, come in!" Hastily he waved her into the workshop. "We've been very worried about you."

That was something new. Merle hadn't experienced someone in the orphanage ever worrying about anyone else. If one of the children vanished, he or she was looked for halfheartedly, usually without success. One burden less, one more place free.

It was warm in the workshop. Steam puffed in little white clouds from Arcimboldo's apparatus, which were linked together with a network of pipes, tubing, and glass globes. The mirror maker used the machines only at night, when he was alone. During the day he busied himself in traditional ways and methods, perhaps because he didn't want to give his pupils any deep insights into the secrets of his art. Did he ever sleep at all? Hard to say. In Merle's eyes Arcimboldo belonged to the fixed inventory of the workshop, just like the oak doors and the high windows with their dust-encrusted panes on which generations of apprentices had scratched their initials.

Arcimboldo walked over to one of the devices, adjusted a switch, and then turned to her. Behind him the machine spurted out three clouds of steam in short bursts. "So now, tell! Where were you?"

Merle had considered all the long way back over what she wanted to say to Arcimboldo. The decision had not been an easy one for her. "I don't think you're going to understand me."

"Don't worry about that. I only want to hear the truth."

She took a deep breath. "I've come to thank you. And so that you know that I'm all right."

"That sounds as though you intend to leave us."

"I'm going away from Venice."

She had reckoned with all possible reactions to this news, such as that he would laugh at her, scold her, or lock her up. But not with the sorrow that now darkened his eyes. No anger, no malice, only plain regret. "What has happened?"

She told him everything. Beginning with her meeting with Serafin, about the fight in the deserted house, the vial with the Flowing Queen, and about Serafin being taken prisoner. She described the robes and faces of the three traitors to him, and he nodded in annoyance at each individual, as if he knew exactly who was the one involved. She spoke of the voice in her head and, a little ashamed, of the fact that she had drunk the contents of the vial.

After she'd finished, Arcimboldo sank dejectedly onto a wooden stool. With a cloth he blotted the sweat from his forehead, blew his nose into it forcefully, and threw it into the stove opening. Both watched as the material was consumed by the flames. They were quiet, almost a little reverent, as if what was burning there was something else: a memory, perhaps, or the thought of what might have been—without the Egyptians, without traitors, and without the poison spell that had driven the Flowing Queen out of the canal.

"You're right," said Arcimboldo after a while. "It's no longer safe for you here. Not anywhere in Venice. But in you the Flowing Queen can leave the lagoon, for you were born here and so are a part of her."

"You know more about her than you've ever told us," she declared.

He smiled sadly. "A little. She was always an important

part of my work. Without her there can be no more magic mirrors."

"But that will mean that . . ."

"That sooner or later I must close the workshop. So it is. The water of the lagoon is a component of my art. Without the breath of the Flowing Queen that goes into every mirror, all my talents are useless."

Apprehension closed around Merle's heart. "What about the others? Junipa and Boro and . . ." There was a lump in her throat. "Must they go back to the orphanages?"

Arcimboldo thought briefly about it, then shook his head. "No, not that. But who knows what will happen when the Egyptians invade? No one can say ahead of time. There will perhaps be fighting. Then the boys will certainly want to fight on the side of the defenders." He rubbed both hands over his face. "As if that would do any good."

Merle wished that the Flowing Queen would give her an answer to that. A few reassuring words, something or other! But the voice inside her kept silent, and she herself didn't know how she could have cheered the mirror maker.

"You must keep on taking care of Junipa," she said. "That you must promise me."

"Certainly." But his agreement didn't sound quite as convincing as Merle wanted it to be.

"Do you think she's in danger from the Egyptians? Because of her eyes?"

"No matter where the Empire has invaded, the first to suffer under them have always been the sick, the wounded, and the weak. The Pharaoh puts healthy men and women into his factories, but the rest . . . I can give you no answer about that, Merle."

"But *nothing* must happen to Junipa!" Merle could no longer understand how she'd thought of going away without saying good-bye to Junipa. She had to see her, as quickly as possible. Perhaps she could even take her with her. . . .

"*No,*" the Flowing Queen weighed in. "*That is impossible.*"

"Why not?" Merle asked rebelliously. Arcimboldo looked up, since he assumed she was speaking to him. But when he realized that her look was directed inward, he knew whom she was addressing.

"*The way we must go is hard enough for one alone. The old man has promised to take care of your friend.*"

"But I—"

"*It will not work.*"

"Don't interrupt me!"

"*You must believe me. Here she is safe. There, outside, she will only bring you into unnecessary danger. Both of you.*"

"Both of us?" retorted Merle acidly. "*You,* you mean!"

"Merle!" Arcimboldo had stood up and taken her by the shoulders. "If you are really speaking with the Flowing Queen, you should adopt a different tone."

"Bah!" She took a step back. Suddenly there were tears in her eyes. "What do you know anyway? Junipa is my friend. I can't just run out on her!"

She took another step and rubbed angrily at her eyes. She didn't want to cry. Not here, not now.

"You aren't running out on me," said a voice behind her, very gently, very softly. Merle whirled around.

"Junipa!"

In the dark of the open door the silvery eyes were sparkling like a pair of stars that had just wandered there from heaven. Junipa walked forward. The yellow flames of the stove fire flickered over her thin features. She was wearing her white nightgown, with a red shawl over it.

"I couldn't sleep," she said. "I was worried about you. Eft came to me and said that I'd find you here."

Dear, good Eft, thought Merle gratefully. She'd never show it openly, but she knows exactly what's going on in each of us.

Relieved, she hugged Junipa. It felt good to see her friend and to hear her voice. It seemed as though they had been separated for weeks, although she'd left Junipa at the festival just a few hours before.

When Merle let go, she looked Junipa straight in the

eyes. They unsettled her no longer; she'd seen worse in the meantime.

"I listened at the door," Junipa confessed with a shadow of a smile. "Eft showed me the best way to do it." She pointed over her shoulder, and there, in the dark of the corridor, stood Eft, who raised an eyebrow but said nothing.

Merle couldn't help it: She laughed, although it wasn't at all how she was feeling. She no longer had herself under control, just laughed and laughed. . . .

"You heard everything," she chortled finally. "Both of you?"

Junipa nodded, while Eft's eyes suggested a smile, but otherwise she remained stock-still.

"Then you certainly think I'm crazy."

"No," said Junipa earnestly. And Eft said softly, "The one touched has come home to take leave. The way of the hero takes its beginning."

Merle didn't feel like a hero, and that this all might be the beginning of something . . . she didn't want to think about that at all. But in her heart she of course knew that Eft was right. A leave-taking, a beginning, and then a journey. Her journey.

Junipa grasped her hand and held it fast. "I'm staying here with Arcimboldo and Eft. You go wherever you must go."

"Junipa, do you remember what you told me, on the very first night?"

"That I was always just a millstone around people's necks?"

Merle nodded. "But you most certainly are not! And you wouldn't be either, if you'd come with me!"

Junipa's smile outshone the cool silver of her eyes. "I know. Much has changed since that night. Arcimboldo can use my help, especially if it really should come to a fight of Venetians against Egyptians. The boys would be the first to join the resistance."

"You have to stop them."

"You know Dario," Arcimboldo said with a sigh. "He won't let anyone keep him out of an ordinary scrap."

"But a war isn't a scrap!"

"He won't see it that way. And Boro and Tiziano will go with him." The mirror maker looked very old and gray, as if the admission of his powerlessness cost him great strength. "Junipa will be a valuable help to us. In all things."

Merle wondered if Arcimboldo perhaps loved Eft the way a man can love a woman. Did he see in Junipa the daughter he and the mermaid would never have?

But who was she anyway that she was trying to evaluate the feelings of another? She'd never had a family, didn't know what it was like to have a father and a mother. Perhaps Junipa would find that out anyhow, if she gave Arcimboldo and Eft a chance.

It was right to go alone. Only she and the Flowing

161

Queen. Junipa's place was here, in this house, with these people.

She pressed her friend to her once more, then embraced Arcimboldo, and finally also Eft. "Farewell," she said. "We'll all see each other again, sometime."

"Do you know the way?" Junipa asked.

"I will show her," said Eft, before Merle could answer at all. Arcimboldo agreed with a nod.

Merle and the mermaid exchanged a look. Eft's eyes gleamed, but perhaps that was only due to the hard contrast with the shadow that the edge of the mask cast over her features.

Junipa grasped Merle's hands one last time. "Good luck," she said, her voice thick. "Take good care of yourself."

"The Flowing Queen is with me." The words were out before Merle could even form the thought of speaking them. She wondered if perhaps the Queen had helped to reassure Junipa.

"Come now," Eft said, and she led the way down the corridor with quick steps.

After a few yards Merle looked around once, back to the door of the workshop. There stood Junipa, beside Arcimboldo. For an irritating moment Merle saw herself standing there at the side of the mirror maker, his arm on her shoulder. But then her likeness turned back into the girl with the mirror eyes, dark hair became blond, her stature still smaller, more vulnerable.

Eft led her out to the inner courtyard, led her straight over to the well, led her down into the depths.

The inside of the well felt like something living, and in spite of the coolness of the stone it grew warm around Merle, and she thought: *Yes, this is how it can begin. This is how it can truly begin.*

7

THROUGH THE CANALS

MERMAIDS! A THRONG OF MERMAIDS!

In the gray-green darkness, a silvery twinkle shone from their tails like the flickering of fireflies on a summer night. Two of them were holding Merle by the hands and pulling her along with them through the canals.

Eft had climbed down into the well along with her. Only very gradually had it become clear to Merle that the gentle murmur around her legs did not come from the water itself. Something was moving around her in the water, whirling rapidly, touching her with featherlight fingers, more delicately even than a dog's nose sniffing a stranger, very carefully, very lightly. She had the feeling the touches reached deep under her skin, as if someone were reading her spirit.

Eft spoke a few words in the strange language of the mer-folk. Alien and mysterious, they echoed from the walls of the well shaft, penetrating deep below the surface to the ears of those who understood and knew what was to be done.

A pale hand appeared out of the water in front of Merle and handed her a globe of veined glass. It appeared to be a kind of helmet. Eft helped her to invert it over her head and to fasten the little leather band firmly around her neck. Merle wasn't at all afraid anymore, not in this place, not among these creatures.

"*I am with you,*" said the Flowing Queen. For her this was a homecoming to her kingdom, imprisoned in Merle's body and yet protected by it from the Egyptian sorcerers' poison.

Eft had remained behind in the well, and now Merle was swimming underwater in a swarm of mermaids through the canals. Where were they taking her? Why was she able to breathe inside the glass globe? And why did the mermaids give off a comfortable warmth so that Merle didn't freeze in the icy water?

Questions upon questions, and new ones kept adding to them, an army of doubts forming in her head.

"*I can give you answers to some,*" said the Flowing Queen.

Merle didn't dare speak, for fear of using up the air in the glass helmet.

"*You do not have to say it for me to hear it,*" said the Flowing Queen in Merle's innermost self. "*I thought you had understood that much already.*"

Merle took pains to formulate her thoughts into clear sentences.

"How long can I breathe under this thing?"

"*As long as you want.*"

"Does Eft use it too when she climbs down into the well at night?"

"*Yes. But it was not created for her. It comes from a time when the merfolk still commanded some of the old knowledge, from ancient times when the water was everywhere and the multiplicity of life in the oceans was immeasurable. Some of that knowledge has remained, buried in the old cities under the sea, in deep trenches and folds on the sea bottom. In those days, countless years ago, expeditions were sent out from the cities from time to time, and sometimes they returned with treasures like this helmet.*"

"Is it technology or magic?"

"*What is magic but technology that most men do not understand—not yet or no longer?*" The Queen seemed to be amused at her own words for a moment, then became serious again. "*But you are not entirely wrong. From your point of view it is a work of magic rather than technology. What looks to you like glass is in reality hardened water.*"

"Arcimboldo said that he used the water of the lagoon for producing his magic mirrors. And that he can only work it when you are contained in it."

"He uses a similar process. Externally his mirrors look as if they consisted of ordinary glass. But in truth their surface is an alloy of hardened water. Centuries ago, in the era of the suboceanic kingdoms, craftsmen worked with water the way you humans today work with wood and metal. Another time, another knowledge! Arcimboldo is one of the few who know how to handle it today—even though his cunning is only a shadow of the suboceanic craftsmen's. And Arcimboldo spoke the truth: It was my presence that made the waters of the lagoon what they were. Without me they will not harden."

Merle nodded thoughtfully. All the Flowing Queen's explanations led to one thing. She hesitated before she directed the thought to the Queen: "Are you a suboceaner? One of the old people under the sea?"

The Queen was silent for a long time, while the shimmering fish tails of the mermaids danced around Merle in the darkness.

"I am old," she said at last. *"Infinitely older than all the life under the sea."*

There was something in the Flowing Queen's tone that made Merle doubt her words. What she said was certainly no lie—but was it the whole truth? Merle knew that the Queen at this moment was reading her thoughts and so also knew her doubt. But for some reason the Queen didn't address it. Instead she changed the subject:

"Before, you wanted to know where the mermaids are taking us."

"Out of the lagoon?"

"No, that they cannot do. The danger would be too great. If an Egyptian lookout were to discover a whole swarm of them under the surface, he would follow them. We cannot risk that. Too many merfolk have died at the hands of men already—I will not ask them to now give their lives for their oppressors as well."

Fascinated, Merle's eyes followed the slender bodies swarming around them and safely guiding them through the deep canals. A reassuring warmth came from the hands of the two mermaids who were gently pulling her through the water.

"They are taking us to the Piazza San Marco," said the Queen.

"But that's—"

"The center of the city. I know."

"And there we'll run straight into the arms of the Guard!"

"Not if I can prevent it."

"It's my body, don't forget! I'm the one who has to run away. And be tortured. And killed."

"There is no other way. There is only one way by which we can leave the city. And to do that, someone must help us."

"In the Piazza San Marco, of all places?"

"We have no other choice, Merle. We can only meet him there. There he is . . . well, he is being held prisoner."

Merle choked on her own breath. Right beside the Piazza San Marco lay the old Doge's palace, the former residence of the Venetian princes and today the domicile of the city councillors. The dungeon of the palace was notorious, as was the one under its lead roofs, and the extensive prison on the other side of the canal, too, which could only be entered from the palace, over the Bridge of Sighs. Whoever crossed that bridge never saw daylight again.

"In all seriousness, you intend to free a prisoner from the Doge's dungeon so that he can help us leave Venice? We might just as well jump from the nearest high tower!"

"That is closer to the truth than you think, Merle. Because the one who will help us is not imprisoned in the dungeon but in the Campanile."

"The highest tower in the city!"

"Indeed."

The Campanile stood on the Piazza San Marco and towered over all of Venice. Merle still did not understand what the Queen was driving at.

"But there's no prison in there!"

"Not for ordinary criminals. Do you remember the legend?"

"What's your friend's name?"

"Vermithrax. But you know him rather as the—"

"The Ancient Traitor!"

"The same."

"But that's only a story! An old wives' tale. Vermithrax never really lived."

"I think he would be of another opinion."

Merle closed her eyes for a few seconds. She had to concentrate, make no mistakes now. Her life depended on it.

Vermithrax, the Ancient Traitor! He was a figure of myth and sayings; people used his name as a curse. But a living, breathing creature—never! Magic spells and mermaids, all that was reality, a part of her everyday world. But Vermithrax? That was as if someone told her he'd had lunch with God.

Or drunk the Flowing Queen.

"All right," said Merle in her thoughts with a sigh, "you're saying, then, that the Ancient Traitor is being held prisoner in the Campanile on the Piazza San Marco, right?"

"My word on it."

"And we're simply going to go to him, free him, and . . . then what?"

"That you will see when we are with him. He still owes me a favor."

"Vermithrax owes you something?"

"A long time ago I helped him."

"That obviously brought him far—straight into prison!"

"Your mockery, my dear, is superfluous."

Merle shook her head in resignation. One of the mermaids looked over to make sure everything was all right. Merle gave her a brief smile. The woman returned it with her shark's smile and turned her eyes forward again.

"If he's been held there all these years, how come no one knows about it?"

"*Oh, everyone knows it.*"

"But they think it's a legend!"

"*Because they want it that way. Perhaps many tales and myths would turn out to be true if only anyone had the courage to look in a well for a golden ball or cut the thorn hedge around a castle.*"

Merle thought it over. "He's really up there?"

"*That he is.*"

"How do you intend to free him? He'll certainly be heavily guarded."

"*With a little luck,*" the Queen replied.

Merle was just about to start an answer when she sensed that the mermaids were rising toward the surface. Above her, Merle could make out the keels of gondolas, rocking gently on the waves; they lay next to each other lined up in rows. Merle knew where they were. This was the gondola landing area at the Piazza San Marco.

The water around the gondolas had taken on an orange glow. *Daybreak,* Merle thought with relief. *Sunrise.* Her mood rose a little, even though the light would make their way to the Campanile more difficult.

"*Too early,*" countered the Flowing Queen. She sounded concerned. "*Too early for sunrise.*"

"But the light!"

"*It is shining toward us from the west. The sun comes up in the east.*"

"What is it then?"

The Flowing Queen was silent for a moment, while the mermaids stopped uncertainly several yards under the surface.

"*Fire,*" she said then. "*The Piazza San Marco is on fire!*"

8

MESSENGER OF FIRE

THREE YARDS ABOVE THE GROUND, THE LION OPENED ITS paws and let him drop. Serafin arched his back in the air and landed safely on his hands and feet, thanks to thousands of similar leaps from high windows, roof balustrades, and terraces. He might no longer be a master thief of the Guild, but he hadn't lost his skills.

In a flash he righted himself, slightly bent forward, ready for battle, when two guardsmen pointed their rifles at him and thus banished any thought of self-defense. Serafin expelled his breath sharply; then he stretched and relaxed his muscles. He was a prisoner; it might be smarter not to act too obstreperous. He would need his powers later, when they brought him before the jailer and his torturers. No need to wear himself out on a few guardsmen.

Resignedly he held out both arms so they could put on the hand irons. Yet the men didn't do it but kept him in check with their rifles. Only a boy. Not worth the trouble.

Serafin suppressed a smile. He wasn't afraid of them. So long as he was still outdoors, outside the dungeon, and far from the Bridge of Sighs, that last walk of the condemned, he had no fear. His self-confidence was a protective shield that he held upright in order not to think of Merle—though he wasn't entirely successful.

Nothing must have happened to her! She was alive and safe! These words became a credo that he repeated in his innermost thoughts.

Concentrate on your surroundings! he said to himself. *And ask yourself questions—for instance, why did we land just here and not in the prison courtyard?*

This was amazing, in fact. The lion had thrown him down on the edge of the Piazza San Marco, where the two guardsmen were already waiting for him. Now they were joined by two more. All four wore the black leather of the Councillors' Guard, ornamented with rivets, which gleamed in the light of some fire beacons marking the shore very close by.

The Piazza San Marco—St. Mark's Square—stretched out in an L-shape in the center of Venice. One end was bounded by the water. The entrance to the Grand Canal was very close by, while on the opposite bank the towers and roofs of the island of Giudecca rose against the night sky.

The piazza was surrounded by splendid buildings. The most impressive was the Basilica of St. Mark, a massive monster of domes and towers. Venetian seafarers had brought together the gold ornaments and the statues from all over the world centuries before. Some called it the house of God, others the pirates' cathedral.

Beside the basilica stretched the facade of the Doge's palace, where no prince had reigned for a long time. Today the city councillors determined the policies of the city, with sumptuous feasting and drinking.

Serafin and his guards were situated on the opposite side of the piazza, at the end of a long arcade, not very far from the water. The nearby columns shielded them from the view of the vendors who, careless of the early hour and the darkness, had already begun to set up their meager displays in the piazza. It was a wonder any trade at all was possible after so many years of siege.

Serafin briefly weighed an attempt to run and plunge into the water. But the guardsmen were quick shots. He wouldn't even make half the distance before their bullets hit him. He must wait for a better opportunity.

Meanwhile, he'd figured out why the lion had brought him here and not to the prison courtyard. His

guards were under the command of the three councillors who were working clandestinely for the Empire
and had betrayed Venice. The other councillors must
not learn of it. But a prisoner who was set down in the
prison by a flying lion of the Guard would doubtless
attract attention. That was exactly what the traitors
must avoid, and so they wanted him to go the last portion of the way on foot. That way he would pass
through as an ordinary criminal whom the guardsmen
had picked up by chance, and especially since some of
them would recognize him as a former master thief of
the Guild.

And if he cried the truth aloud? If he told anyone on
his path, anyone here on the piazza, what he'd seen? Then
he could—

His head was brutally jerked backward. Hands shoved
coarse material in his mouth, pulled the edges over his
chin and nose, and knotted the ends at the back of his
head. The gag was so tight that it hurt. Also, the taste was
anything but pleasant.

So much for his—admittedly not very well thought-out—
plan.

With their gun barrels the men poked him out from the
shadows of the arcade into the piazza. A peculiar smell
hung in the air. Possibly it was wafting over from the
palace dungeons.

Others also seemed to be aware of the stench. A few

vendors looked up in irritation from their work on their stands, sniffing the air and making faces.

Serafin tried to get a look at his guards. But when he turned his head to the side, someone slammed a rifle butt into the small of his back. "Eyes forward!"

The traders' stands were arranged in two rows to form a shopping street that ran from the water's edge toward the Basilica of San Marco. Serafin's path crossed it in the middle of the piazza. Now he could see more clearly some of the men and women who were unloading their goods there in the light of the torches and gas lanterns. There might still be more than an hour left till sunrise; but then they would be all prepared for the buyers.

Serafin observed that increasingly fewer salespeople were busy with their stands. Some had grouped together, gesticulating wildly in the air and wrinkling their noses. "Sulfur," he heard over and over. "Why sulfur? And why here?"

He must have been mistaken. The stench was not coming from the dungeon.

They now passed the second shopping row and left the stands behind them. There were still about a hundred yards to the narrow side entrance to the Doge's palace. Other guardsmen were standing watch to the right and left of it. Among them was a captain of the Guard, with the symbol of the flying lion decorating his black uniform. Frowning, he observed the approach of Serafin and his escort.

The talk of the dealers at Serafin's back grew louder, more excited, more confused. Serafin felt as though there were a sudden trembling in the air. His skin began to prickle.

Someone screamed. A single, sharp cry, not even particularly loud. The captain of the Guard at the gate turned his gaze from Serafin to the center of the piazza. The smell of sulfur was now so strong that it hit Serafin in the stomach. Out of the corner of his eye he saw that his guards were holding their noses; the stench was much stronger for them than it was for him. The gag over his mouth and nose protected him from the worst of it.

One of the men stopped and vomited. Then a second.

"Stop!" commanded one of the soldiers. After a brief hesitation, Serafin turned around.

Two of his guards were doubled over and coughing and spitting vomit on their shining polished boots. A third was holding his hand over his mouth. Only the fourth, the one who'd ordered him to stop, was still holding his weapon pointed at Serafin.

Beyond the guardsmen Serafin saw the groups of dealers spring apart. Some of them were staggering around blindly, stamping through puddles of vomit. Serafin glanced back at the side door of the Doge's palace. There, too, the guards were battling with their nausea. Only the captain was still standing up straight; he was holding his nose with one hand. Alternately he breathed through his mouth and screamed orders to which no one was paying any attention.

In silence Serafin thanked his guards for the gag. He felt sick too, but the material kept the worst of the sulfurous fog away from him.

While he was considering whether this was the opportunity he'd been waiting for, a deep rumbling began. The ground trembled. The rumbling grew louder and increased to a thundering.

One of the stands in the center caught fire. Panicked dealers started a wild Saint Vitus's dance around the flames. A second wall of planking flamed up, then a third. Like the wind, the flames rushed along the shopping street, even where the individual stands stood far away from each other, as if the fire might have reached over to them on its own. There was no wind blowing that could have fanned the flames, yet they kept on spreading. The air was still except for that imperceptible trembling that raised the hairs on Serafin's forearms.

The captain of the Guard looked over at the seething waters, scanning for enemy gunboats or fire catapults. Nothing, no attacker. Serafin followed his eyes to the sky. There, too, only darkness, no sunbarks of the Empire.

The two rows of booths were now ablaze, a flickering beacon that cast the facade of the palace and the basilica in firelight. The screaming dealers made no attempt at all to save their goods. In their panic they fell back to the left and right to the edges of the piazza.

Serafin drew in a deep breath—sulfur, still more sulfur!—and then he ran. He was ten paces away before one of his guards noticed his disappearance. It was the one who'd vomited first; he was just wiping a hand over his lips. With the other he held his rifle and was waving it wildly in Serafin's direction. Now his comrades also looked up and saw their prisoner escaping. One of them pulled his rifle around, aimed, and fired. The bullet whistled past Serafin's ear. Before the man could shoot a second time, a new wave of sickness overwhelmed him. A second man fired, but his bullet came nowhere near Serafin. Way before its target, the shot drilled a scar in the pavement, a golden crater in the flickering light of the fire.

Serafin ran as fast as he could, although he was soon out of breath. Nevertheless, he didn't pull down the gag. He stormed over to the basilica and only dared to turn around once he was there. No one was following him. His guards were busy with themselves, one supporting himself on his rifle like a crutch. Some vendors were also crouching on the ground, far from the flames, their faces buried in their hands. Others had sought protection behind the columns of the arcade and stared numbly over at the flickering inferno that was consuming their possessions.

But the thundering sounded once more, this time so loud that everyone clapped their hands over their ears.

Serafin took cover behind a flower tub, one of the many that flanked the basilica. It would certainly have been more sensible to flee and disappear into one of the alleyways. But he couldn't run away now. He had to see what happened next.

At first it seemed as if all the burning dealers' booths collapsed in on themselves at once. Only then could Serafin see the true extent of the catastrophe.

Between the flickering rows of stands, exactly along the lane between them, the ground had opened. The fissure extended for a length of 100 or 120 yards. It was broad enough to swallow the stands along its edges.

Serafin stopped breathing, incapable of thinking of anything else, not even of his flight. The guardsmen had drawn together, just in front of the gate of the palace, and there they stood like an indignant herd of geese, yelling in wild confusion and waving their weapons, while their captain tried in vain to reestablish order.

Serafin crouched lower behind the flower tub until only his eyes peered over the edge.

Flames were flickering within the fissure. At first they seemed to burn evenly, then they moved gradually from both ends toward the middle, and there they pulled themselves together into an unbearably bright ball of flame.

A figure peeled itself out of the firelight.

It floated upright and bore something around its head that at first sight looked like a halo. The appearance was reminiscent of the representations of Christ on altarpieces, images as he ascended to heaven after his death, the hands crossed gracefully. But then Serafin saw that the figure had the face of a newborn, fleshy and swollen. The halo revealed itself to be a sort of circular saw blade, with teeth as long as Serafin's thumbs; it was attached to the back of the creature's head and appeared to be fused with skin and bone. The crossed hands were gigantic chicken claws, gray and scaly and segmented. The creature's plump body ended not in legs but in something long, pointed, that was wound with wet bandages; it looked like a trembling reptile's tail, which was prevented by the bandaging from thrashing around uncontrollably. The creature's swollen eyelids slid back like night snails and exposed pitch-black eyeballs. Also, the blubbery lips opened, revealing teeth filed to a point.

"Hell presents its greetings," intoned the creature. Its voice sounded like a child's, only louder, more penetrating. It echoed over the whole piazza.

The guardsmen raised their rifles, but the messenger from Hell laughed at them. He was now hovering six feet over the fiery crack, and still its flames bathed him in garish flickering light. Tiny tongues of fire danced up and down along the bandages of his lower body, without burning the material.

"Citizens of this city," cried the emissary so loudly that his voice even carried over the crackling. "My masters have an offer to make you." Green spittle poured from the corners of his mouth, spread itself into the folds of his double chin, collected on his crop, and dropped down below. The heat of the flames evaporated the drops as they fell.

"We wish," he said, and he bowed, with a crooked grin, "to be your friends from now on."

Something shook the world.

Just a moment before, the swarm of mermaids had been quietly floating in the water several yards under the surface. Then an earsplitting bang had sounded, and a shock wave seized them and whirled them around in confusion, as if an angry god had hit the sea with a fist. Merle saw the gondolas over them being thrown against each other like paper boats; some were wedged together, others broke into pieces. Suddenly an invisible force tore her away from the two mermaids holding her hands. First she was sucked down deeper below, and then spat up again into a dense jumble of gondola pieces. She opened her eyes wide, saw the sharp keels rushing toward her like black sword blades, was about to scream—

The round helmet of hardened water took the blow. A hard jolt went through Merle's body, but the pain was bearable. The water was as roiled as if a hurricane were storming over the surface. Suddenly a mermaid's hands grasped her by the waist from behind and swiftly maneuvered her under the gondolas and through to the pilings of a nearby boat landing, only a few yards away. The mermaid's face was strained. It was costing her all her strength to withstand the alternating play of pressure and suction. Merle reached the pier and before she could react, she was catapulted to the surface, in her head the Flowing Queen's scream, *"Hold on tight!"*

She threw open her arms and clung to a slimy pile of the landing stage, slipping down it a little ways until her thrashing feet found a toehold. In no time she clambered up onto the steps, collapsed onto the dock, and coughed up saltwater.

The surface of the water around the landing was still turbulent, but it seemed to be quieting gradually. Merle took off the helmet, saw a hand stretching out to her from the waves in farewell, and threw the sphere into the water. Delicate fingers closed around the edge of the neck opening and pulled the helmet into the depths. Merle watched a swarm of bright bodies shoot away under the water.

"I feel something . . . ," the Queen began slowly, but then she fell silent again almost immediately.

Merle turned and looked over through dripping strands of hair to the piazza.

At first she saw only the fire.

Then the figure. She saw it as clearly as if every detail, every horrible detail, had burned into her retina within the space of a second.

". . . be your friends from now on," she heard the creature saying.

She picked herself up and ran onto the pavement. But there she stood still. She hesitated. Guardsmen were gingerly gathering around the hovering creature, way beyond its reach, yet still close enough to reach it with their bullets.

Hell's messenger paid no attention to the soldiers but directed his words to his audience behind the columns of the arcade and around the edges of the piazza.

"Common folk of Venice, Hell offers you a pact." Luxuriating, he allowed the words to reverberate. The echo transformed his child's voice into a grotesque squeal. "Your masters, the councillors of this city, have rejected our offer. Yet hear it yourselves and come to your own decision." Again he allowed a pause, punctuated by commands of the captain of the Guard. A second, then a third troop hurried forward as reinforcements, accompanied by a dozen riders on stone lions.

"You fear the wrath of the Pharaoh's kingdom," the messenger continued. "And that rightly. More than thirty years long you have warded off the Empire. Yet very soon now the mummy armies of the Pharaoh will launch a great blow and sweep you from the face of the earth. Unless it should happen . . . yes, unless it should happen that you have powerful allies on your side. Allies like my masters!" A pant worked its way through the fleshy lips. "The hosts of our kingdom are a match for those of the Empire. We can protect you. Yes, that we can."

Merle appeared to be spellbound by the disgusting appearance of the fiery figure. More and more people were streaming to the edges of the piazza from all directions, lured by the flames, the noise, and the prospect of a gigantic spectacle.

"We have no time to waste," said the Flowing Queen. *"Quick, run to the Campanile!"*

"But the fire . . ."

"If you run past on the left, you will make it. Please, Merle—this is the best possible moment!"

Merle ran. The tower rose in the inner corner of the L-shaped piazza. She had to run along the entire length of the fiery fissure, behind the messenger from Hell, who was floating over the flames with his face toward the palace. The stench of sulfur was overpowering. The messenger continued, but Merle scarcely heard him. At first, going along with the offer from the princes of Hell might seem appealing—but just looking at the nauseating creature was enough to make it clear that such a pact would take the Venetians from frying pan to fire. True, it might succeed in beating the Empire and keeping it out of the lagoon. But what new governors would seize the palaces of the city instead of the sphinx commanders? And what sacrifices would they require?

Half the distance to the Campanile was behind her before Merle realized that the entrance was unguarded. The tower guards had joined the troops in front of the

Doge's palace. At least a hundred rifle barrels were now pointed at the messenger, and new ones were being added every minute. The lions on the ground, all wingless and of granite, pawed angrily, their claws scratching furrows in the pavement of the piazza. Their riders were having trouble keeping them in check.

"From every inhabitant of the city a drop of blood," cried Hell's messenger into the crowd. "Only one drop from each, and the pact is sealed. Citizens of Venice, think! How much blood will the Empire demand of you? How many of you will die in fighting around the lagoon, and how many dead will the hosts of the Pharaoh later claim?"

A young boy, seven years old at the most, tore himself loose from his horrified mother and ran on his short legs past the soldiers up to the messenger.

"The Flowing Queen protects us!" he cried up to the creature. "We don't need your help!"

The panicked mother tried to run after him, but others held her fast. She struggled, flailed around her, but she could not get free. She cried the name of her child over and over again.

The boy looked defiantly up at the messenger once more. "The Flowing Queen will always protect us!" Then he simply turned around and ran back to the others without the messenger's hurting him at all.

Merle had felt a pain in her chest at the child's words. It was a moment before she realized that it wasn't her own feeling. It was the pain of the Flowing Queen, her despair, her shame.

"*They are relying on me,*" she said tonelessly. "*They are all relying on me. And I have disappointed them.*"

"They don't have any idea of what has happened."

"*They will soon find out. At the latest when the Pharaoh's war galleys anchor in the lagoon and the sunbarks spray fire from the sky.*" She was silent for a moment, then added, "*They should accept the messenger's offer.*"

Merle almost stumbled over her own feet in fright. Only twenty more yards to the tower.

"What?" she cried out. "Are you serious?"

"*It is a possibility.*"

"But . . . Hell! I mean, what do we know about it?" And she added quickly, "Professor Burbridge's exploration experiences alone are enough to . . . oh, well, wish them to the Devil."

"*It is a possibility,*" the Queen said again. Her voice was unusually flat and weak. The little boy's words seemed to have touched her deeply.

"A pact with the Devil is never a possibility," contradicted Merle, gasping for air. Running and arguing demanded too much of her stamina. "The old stories have already told us that. Everyone who's gotten himself into something like that is the loser in the end. Everyone!"

"*Again, they are only stories, Merle. Do you know whether anyone really ever tried it?*"

Merle looked back over her shoulder at the messenger in the midst of the flames. "Look at him! And now don't give me wise sayings, like 'You shouldn't judge a person by his looks'! He isn't even a human being!"

"*I am not one either.*"

Staggering, Merle reached the door of the Campanile. It was standing open. "Listen," she gasped, exhausted, "I don't want to insult you, but Hell—" She broke off, shaking her head. "Perhaps you really aren't human enough to understand about that."

With that she gave herself a shake and entered the tower.

Serafin could have seen Merle running on the other side of the piazza, but his eyes were firmly fixed on the messenger—and on the ever-increasing crowd of soldiers gathering in front of him.

The part of the Piazza San Marco directly in front of the basilica was now also filled with people who had hurried there from everywhere to see what was going on. Some might already have heard that a messenger from Hell had appeared, but probably they hadn't believed it. Now they could see the truth with their own eyes.

Serafin kept fighting the urge to just run away. He'd only escaped prison by a hair, and now with every minute he spent here, the danger increased that someone would recognize him and take him prisoner. It was dumb, so dumb to hide here behind the flower tub while the Guard were looking for him!

But the soldiers had other concerns at the moment, and Serafin, too, pushed out of his mind the danger he was in. He must see with his own eyes how this matter ended, he must hear what the messenger had to say.

And now he caught sight of something else: Three men had come out of the palace. Three councillors in splendid robes. Purple, scarlet, and gold. The traitors. The councillor in gold ran up to the captain of the Guard and was talking excitedly to him.

The flames flickered higher for a moment, caressing the body of the messenger with their glowing tongues and illuminating the smile that divided his jellylike features.

"One drop of blood," he cried. "Think carefully about it, citizens of Venice! Only one drop of blood!"

Merle was rushing up the steps of the Campanile. She was gasping for air. Her heart pounded as though it were going to burst in her chest. She couldn't remember when she had ever been so exhausted.

"What do you know about the Ancient Traitor?" the Flowing Queen asked.

"Only what everyone knows. The old story."

"He never really was a traitor. Not the way they tell it."

Merle had trouble getting enough breath to speak; even listening was giving her problems.

"I will tell you what really happened. Back in that time when Vermithrax was turned into the Ancient Traitor," the Flowing Queen went on. *"But first you should know what he is."*

"And . . . what . . . is . . . he?" Merle gasped, as she took step after step.

"Vermithrax is a lion. One of the old ones."

"A . . . lion?"

"A flying and talking lion." The Queen stopped speaking for a moment. *"At least he was when I saw him last."*

Merle stopped in astonishment. She had a terrible stitch in her side. "But . . . lions don't talk!"

"Not any that you know. But earlier, a long time ago, many years before the revival of the Pharaoh and the era of the mummy wars, all lions could talk. They flew higher and faster than the great sea eagles, and their songs were more beautiful than those of men and of the merfolk."

"What happened?" Merle started moving again, but she wasn't able to manage more than a weary dragging forward. She was still dripping wet and completely exhausted and although she was sweating, her entire body shivered.

"The stone lions and the people of Venice have been allies since time immemorial. No one knows anymore how this happened originally. Perhaps they were creatures from a distant corner of the world? Or the work of a Venetian alchemist? It doesn't matter. The lions served the Venetians

as fighters in many wars, they accompanied their ships on dangerous trade routes along Africa's coast, and they protected the city with their lives. In thanks, their faces soon appeared on all arms and flags of the city, and they were given an island in the north end of the lagoon as a home city."

"If the lions were so strong and powerful, why didn't they build their own city?" Merle could hardly hear her own words, so weakly did they pass her lips.

"Because they trusted the citizens of Venice and felt bound to them. Trust was always an important part of their nature. The wanted it no other way. Their bodies might be of stone, their flight fast, and their songs full of poetry, yet no one had ever seen a lion build a house. They had long accustomed themselves to existence among men who loved roofs over their heads and the comfort of a city. And that, I fear, was the reason for their downfall."

Merle paused briefly at a narrow window that looked out on the piazza. She was alarmed when she saw that the numbers of soldiers and guardsmen had multiplied within the last few minutes. Obviously the councillors had pulled together the uniformed services from all quarters, from the night sentries to the highly decorated captain. There must be hundreds. And they were all pointing their rifles and revolvers, even brandishing unsheathed sabers, at the messenger from Hell.

"Keep on going! Hurry!"

After Merle, sighing, had turned to the stairs again, the Queen continued her story: *"It could not go well. Humans are not created to exist peacefully with other creatures. It happened as it must. It began with fear. Fear of the strength of the lions, of their powerful wings, their fangs, and their mighty claws. More and more, men forgot how much the lions had done for them, yes, that Venice had them alone to thank for her dominant position in the Mediterranean. From fear grew hatred and from hatred the desire to finally subjugate the lions—for do without them they could not and would not. Under the pretext of preparing a festival of gratitude for the lions, they induced them to gather on their island. Ships transported countless numbers of cattle and swine there, slaughtered and gutted. The slaughterhouses had received the order to put everything they had in their storerooms at the disposal of the festival. In addition there was wine from the best Italian grapes and clear well water from the rocks of the Alps. For two days and two nights the lions enjoyed themselves unrestrainedly on their island. But then, gradually, the sleeping potion with which the treacherous Venetians had painted the meat and with which they had laced the water and the wine took effect. On the third day there was no longer a single lion on his feet in all the lagoon; all had fallen into a deep sleep. And again the butchers went to work, and this time they took from the lions their wings!"*

"They . . . just . . . cut off—"

"Cut off. Indeed. The lions noticed nothing, so powerful was the sleeping potion in their blood. Their wounds were tended to, so that hardly any died, but then the Venetians left them on the island, in the certainty that the weakened lions were prisoners. Lions fear the water, as you know, and the few who tried to leave the island by swimming drowned in the currents."

Merle felt such revulsion that she stopped moving again. "Why are we going to such trouble to save the city? After all that the Venetians have done to the lions and the merfolk! They don't deserve anything better than for the Egyptians to invade here and raze everything to the ground."

She felt the Queen smiling gently, a wonderful warmth in the area of her stomach. *"Don't be so bitter, little Merle. You are also a Venetian, just like many others who do not know all that. The treachery against the lions is long ago, many generations."*

"And you really think people today are wiser?" Merle asked scornfully.

"No. They probably never will be that. But you cannot condemn anyone for a crime that he himself is not responsible for."

"And what about the mermaids, then, that they harness before their boats? Eft said that they all would die."

The Flowing Queen said nothing for a moment. *"If*

more of you knew of that, if more might know the truth . . .
perhaps then there would not be such injustice any longer."

"You say that you are no human—and yet you are
defending us. Just where do you get this damned goodness?"

"*Damned goodness?*" repeated the Queen with amusement. "*Only a human could use those two words in the
same sentence. Perhaps that is one of the reasons I still have
hope for you. But do you not want to hear how the story of
the lions continues? We are almost to the top of the tower.
Before we get there you should know what role
Vermithrax played in all this.*"

"Go on."

"*The lions only recovered slowly, and there were fights
among them as to how to proceed. It was clear they were
prisoners on their own island. They were weak, the pain in
their shoulders threatened to kill them, and they were
despairing. The Venetians offered to supply them with food,
as long as the lions were willing to serve them as slaves. After
long debate, the lion folk agreed to it. Some of them were
transported to another island, where scientists and
alchemists began to undertake experiments with them. New
generations of stone lions were bred until finally they
became what they are today—not animals but also not exact
likenesses of their noble forefathers, a race of lions who were
born without wings and had forgotten their singing.*"

"And what about Vermithrax?" asked Merle. "Or the
lions who can still fly even today?"

"When the Venetians began their treachery, there was a small troop of lions outside the lagoon, spying out the lands to the east for the humans. On their return home they found out what had happened and they roared with rage. But in spite of their anger there were too few of them to offer the Venetians more than a skirmish. So they decided to go away, instead of choosing certain extinction fighting a superior force. There were not more than a dozen, but they flew the entire way across the Mediterranean to the south, and farther still into the heart of Africa. There they lived for a while among the lions of the savannahs, before they realized they were only accepted out of fear rather than as equals. The stone lions retreated farther, high into the mountains of the hot countries, and there they remained for a long time. The injustice of the Venetians became history, then myth. But finally, several hundred years ago, there was a young lion by the name of Vermithrax. He believed all the old legends, and his heart was heavy with grief at the fate of his people. He made the decision to return here in order to pay the citizens of Venice back for their crime. But only a few wanted to join him, for meanwhile the mountains had become homeland to the descendents of the refugees, and hardly any felt pleasure at the thought of heading off into the unknown distance.

"So it happened that Vermithrax made his way to Venice with only a handful of companions. He firmly believed that the oppressed lions of the city would join his side and their tormentors would go down in defeat. But Vermithrax started with a serious error: He underestimated the power of time."

"The power of time?" Merle asked wonderingly.

"Yes, Merle. Time had slowly healed the wounds, and, worse still, had made the lions submissive. The old urge for comfort had overcome the silent, wingless race of lions. They were content with their existence as servants of the Venetians. None of them remembered the life of freedom anymore; the capabilities of their forebears had long been forgotten. Hardly any were willing to put their lives on the line for a rebellion that was not theirs. They obeyed the orders of their human masters rather than rebelling against them. Vermithrax's attack on the city cost many lives and left an entire district in rubble and ashes, but in the long run it was finally doomed to failure. His own people stood against him. It was lions who vanquished him, those lions he would have freed and who now of their free will had become the accomplices of men."

"But then they were really the traitors, not he!"

"All a question of point of view. To the Venetians, Vermithrax was a murderer who had fallen upon them from a foreign sky, killed countless people, and tried to stir up the lions against them. In their view, what they did was completely justifiable. They killed most of the attackers, but they left a few living to allow the scientists to breed a new generation of flying lions. No one remembered any-more how it had been when the lions had wings, and so it seemed alluring to the humans to have winged lion ser-vants who could carry great burdens or, in war, could attack the enemy from the air, the way Vermithrax had done during his attacks on the city. A small number of new lions arose, a cross of the free, winged lions returning home from Africa and the will-less, loyally devoted slaves of Venice. What came out of it you know: the flying lions on which the bodyguards of the city councillors ride today. You have already made their acquaintance."

"And Vermithrax?"

"For Vermithrax they invented a particularly subtle, cruel punishment. Instead of killing him, they imprisoned him in this tower. He must suffer his fate here in the airy heights, and nothing is worse for a flying lion than to be robbed of his ability to fly. For Vermithrax, who had floated free over the broad grasslands of Africa for many years, it was doubly cruel. And so his will was broken—not through the defeat but through the betrayal of his fellow lions. He did not understand the indifference in their hearts, their doglike devotion, and the carelessness with which they had placed themselves under the command of men against him. The knowledge of this betrayal was the hardest of all punishments for him, and so he decided that it was time to put an end to his life. He waved away the food they brought him, not for fear of poison but in the *hope of dying quickly. But Vermithrax, this rebel and rowdy, was probably the first of his race who had to learn that a creature of stone needs no nourishment. Certainly, stone lions also feel hunger and, indeed, eating is one of their favorite activities—but food is not a necessity of life for them. So Vermithrax is still housed in this tower today, over us, under the roof. From there he can look out over the city and is still a prisoner."* The Flowing Queen paused, and then she added, *"To be honest, I do not know what condition we are going to find him in."*

Merle was approaching the last landing. Light fell through a window onto a mighty door of steel. The surface shimmered bluish. "How did you meet Vermithrax?"

"When he led his companions here from Africa several hundred years ago, he thought that he must do the same as men in one thing, in order to be equal to them—he must overcome the inborn fear lions have of the water. His forefathers had become slaves because they could not deal with the waters of the lagoon. They had become prisoners on their own island, and Vermithrax did not want to fall into the same trap as they had. As soon as he saw the lagoon before him, he therefore took heart and plunged into the waters, defying death. But before this challenge even the most daring among the lions must capitulate. The water and the cold numbed him, and he was in danger of drowning."

"And you saved him?"

"I explored his mind as he sank into the deep. I saw the

boldness of his plan and admired his strong will. A plan like that should not have come to grief before it had ever begun. So I called the merfolk to pull him back to the surface and bring him safely to the shore of an uninhabited island. I also introduced myself, and while he returned to himself again and gathered strength, we had long discussions. I will not say that we became friends—for that he understood too little what I really was, and I believe he feared me because I—"

"Because you are water itself?"

"I am the lagoon. I am the water. I am the source of the merfolk. But Vermithrax was a fighter, a hothead with an indomitable will. He showed me respect, and gratitude, but also fear."

The Flowing Queen fell silent as Merle, exhausted, stepped onto the highest landing of the stairs. The steel door of the tower room was three times as high as she was and almost twelve feet wide. Two bolts the length of a man were fastened across the outside.

"How shall we—," she began, but she broke off as the noise on the piazza increased from one moment to the next. She ran to the barred window and looked down.

From here she had a breathtaking view over the front part of the piazza and the fiery fissure opened down its middle, and for the first time she saw that it ended just a few yards before the water. Had the crack continued on into the sea, Merle and the mermaids would have been drawn right into the flames by the suction of the water.

But it wasn't this realization that froze the blood in her veins. It was the catastrophe that was beginning down below.

Three winged lions zoomed down from the roof of the Doge's palace, whipped on by the screams of their riders. The City Council had made its decision: No more dealings with the princes of Hell, once and for all.

Before the messenger could react, the three lions were upon him. Two rushed past him on the left and right, missing him by a hairsbreadth, and were through the flames too quickly for their riders to come to any harm. But the third lion, the one in the middle of the formation, seized the messenger in its open jaws, managing to grab him in the middle of his fat body, snatched him away from the flaming fissure, and carried him off. The messenger shrieked, a dreadful succession of sounds, inconceivably high and shrill for human ears. He was hanging horizontally in the lion's jaws, his bandaged, wormlike lower body twisting like a fat maggot. All over the piazza people cowered; even soldiers let their weapons fall and pressed their hands over their ears.

With the messenger in his mouth, the lion flew a tight curve over the roofs. Then he shot down toward the soldiers gathered in front of the palace. Over their heads, he let the screeching creature drop like a rotten piece of meat.

"*Merle!*" cried the Flowing Queen in her thoughts. "*Merle, the door!...*"

But Merle could not take her eyes off the spectacle. The soldiers sprang apart, just quickly enough to avoid the messenger's falling on their heads. Screaming, he hit the ground among them, robbed of all his loftiness, only a monstrous thing whose gigantic chicken claws thrashed ceaselessly in the air while the worm projection of his lower body drummed in panic on the pavement.

"*Merle!...*"

For a few heartbeats, stillness reigned over the entire piazza. The people were silent, forgetting to breathe, unable to grasp what was happening before their eyes.

Then a triumphant shout went up. The mob had tasted blood. No one thought of the consequences any longer. Almost four decades of isolation and fear of the world outside cleared the way.

Words formed from the shouting, then a shriller, more thundering speech-song:

"Kill the beast! Kill the beast!"

"*Merle! We have no time!*"

"Kill the beast!"

"*Please!*"

"Kill the beast!"

The gash the messenger's fall had opened in the formation of soldiers closed in a wave of pressing bodies, flashing blades, and twisted faces. Dozens of arms rose and fell, striking with sabers, rifle butts, and bare fists at the creature on the ground. The messenger's screaming became a whimper, then was silenced altogether.

"The door, Merle!"

When Merle turned around, in a daze, her eyes fell again on the two powerful bolts. So huge!

"You must open it now," entreated the Queen.

From the other side of the steel came the roar of a lion.

9

THE ANCIENT TRAITOR

THERE WAS NO POINT IN QUESTIONING THE MATTER ANY longer. Merle had undertaken a task. The decision had been made when she drank the contents of the vial, and perhaps even earlier, when she left the lantern festival with Serafin. An adventure—that was what she'd wanted.

It was surprisingly easy to slide back the lower bolt on the door. At first she applied her whole weight against it, but then the gigantic steel bolt slid to the left as if it had just been oiled the day before.

The second bolt was somewhat more difficult. It was fastened a good handsbreadth above Merle's head, too high for her to put her whole weight against it. It took a long time before she finally succeeded in moving it a little bit. Sweat was pouring down her face. The Flowing Queen was silent.

There—the bolt slid to the left. Finally!

"You have to push both doors in," the Queen instructed. She didn't sound really relieved yet. Soldiers were going to be turning up again soon. They had to have Vermithrax freed by that time.

Merle hesitated only long enough to draw a breath. Then she leaned with both hands against the steel doors. With a metallic grinding, the two sides of the door swung inward.

The Campanile's tower room was bigger than she'd expected. In the darkness she could make out the outlines of the jumble of beams that supported the high point of the roof. Far, far above her fluttered pigeons. White bird droppings covered the floorboards like fine snow; it was so dry and dusty that Merle's feet stirred up small clouds with each step. The stale air smelled acrid with the pigeons' excrement. The inhabitant of this attic prison, on the other hand, possessed no scent of his own, nothing that could be differentiated from the stone all around him.

It was very dark. A single shaft of light fell through a window halfway between the floor and the lower timbers of the tower roof. Outside, the sun was finally rising. Bars as thick as Merle's thighbone cut the light into slices.

The walls were covered with a network of steel grating too, as if people were afraid that otherwise the prisoner could tear the walls apart. Even the high roof beams were covered over with gratings.

The light that came in through the window moved like a bundle of gleaming ropes through the tower room and pooled in the center of the floor. On each side of the yellow spot of light, the darkness was total; the opposite wall was not discernible.

Merle felt small and lost under the high arch. What should she do now? she wondered.

"You must greet him. He must know that we come in peace."

"He won't recognize you if you don't speak to him yourself," retorted Merle.

"Oh yes, he will."

"Umm . . . hello?" she said softly.

Pigeons rustled in the joists.

"Vermithrax?"

Rustling sounded. Beyond the sunbeams. Deep in the darkness.

"Vermithrax? I'm here to—"

She broke off as the shadows gathered into something solid, substantial. There was a swishing sound followed by a strong gust of wind—wings that had been folded together, stretching. Then steps, soft, like the padding of cats' paws, not so heavy and jarring as those of the other lions. Animal, and yet placed with deliberation. Cautious.

"The Flowing Queen is with me," she blurted. Probably Vermithrax would laugh at her.

A silhouette, higher than a horse and twice as wide, detached itself from the darkness. In a moment he was standing there in the light, his head bathed in the glow of the morning sun.

"Vermithrax," Merle exhaled softly.

The Ancient Traitor looked at her from proud eyes. His right paw extended murderous claws—and immediately withdrew them again. A flash of quick, hundredfold deaths. Each of his paws was as big as Merle's head, his teeth as long as her finger. His mane, although of stone, rustled and waved at every movement like silky fur.

"Who are you?" His voice was deep and possessed a slight resonance.

"Merle," she said uncertainly. And then again, "I am called Merle. I'm a student of Arcimboldo."

"And bearer of the Flowing Queen."

"Yes."

Vermithrax took a majestic step toward her. "You have opened the door. Are soldiers waiting outside to kill me?"

"At the moment they're all down in the piazza. But they'll be here soon. We have to hurry."

He remained standing there, and now the light illuminated his entire body.

Merle had never before seen a lion of obsidian. He was

raven black, from his nose to his bushy tail. A slight gleam showed on his flanks, the slender back, and his lion's face. The hair of his enormous mane appeared to be constantly in motion, an imperceptible rippling, even when he was holding his head still. His opened wings soared over him, each almost nine feet long. Now he folded them casually together, completely silently. Only a draft of wind again.

"Hurry." Lost in thought, he repeated her last word.

Merle felt impatience rising in her. Lion more or lion less, she didn't want to die just because he couldn't decide whether to trust her.

"Yes, hurry," she said firmly.

"Hold out your hand to him."

"Are you serious?"

The Queen didn't answer, and so with a heavy heart, Merle moved toward the obsidian lion. He awaited her, motionless. Just as she stretched out her hand to him, he raised his right paw in a gliding movement, high enough for it to rest under Merle's fingers.

From one heartbeat to the next a change took place in him. His expression became gentler.

"Flowing Queen," he murmured, scarcely audibly, and inclined his head.

"He can feel you?" Merle asked, without saying it aloud.

"Stone lions are perceptive creatures. He already felt my presence when you opened the door. Otherwise you would have been dead long ago."

Again the lion spoke, and this time his dark eyes fixed on Merle—for the first time, really on *her*. "And your name is Merle?"

She nodded.

"A beautiful name."

There's no time for that now, she wanted to say. But she only nodded again.

"Do you think you can ride on my back?"

Naturally she'd suspected that it would come to that. But now, when a ride on a real stone lion—and in addition, one who could speak and fly—was immediately before her, she felt her knees as weak and fragile as an air bubble.

"You need have no fear," said Vermithrax loudly. "Just hold on tight."

She walked up to him hesitantly and watched as he lay down.

"*Get on with it,*" urged the Queen gruffly.

Merle gave a soundless sigh and swung onto his back. To her amazement the obsidian felt warm beneath her and appeared to fit the form of her legs. She sat as securely as if in a saddle.

"Where shall I hold on?"

"Grab deep into my mane," said Vermithrax. "As deep and as firmly as you can."

"Won't that hurt you?"

He laughed softly and a little bitterly, but he didn't

answer. Merle took hold. The mane of the lion felt neither like real fur nor like stone. Firm, and yet flexible, like the branches of an underwater plant.

"If it comes to a fight," said the lion, looking fixedly over at the door, "bend as deep as you can over my neck. On the ground I'll try to protect you with my wings."

"All right." Merle tried to keep her trembling voice under control, but she succeeded only with difficulty.

Vermithrax began to move and glided to the door in a feline motion. In a flash he was out through the gap between the doors, onto the upper landing of the staircase. He carefully evaluated the width of the stairwell, nodded in satisfaction, and spread his wings.

"Couldn't we run down the steps?" Merle asked worriedly.

"Hurry, you said." Vermithrax hadn't finished speaking when he rose gently in the air, glided over the banister, and plunged steeply into the depths.

Merle let out a high scream as the rushing air pressed on her eyelids and she almost catapulted backward off the lion's body. But then she felt a steady pressure on her back—Vermithrax's tail tip pressed her into his mane from behind.

Her stomach seemed to turn inside out. They fell and fell and fell. . . . The ground in the center of the stairwell was filling her entire field of vision when, with a shake, the obsidian lion righted himself again, swept just over the bottom of the tower, and with an elementally powerful roar, shot out the door of the Campanile, a black streak of stone, larger, harder, heavier than any cannonball and with the force of a hurricane.

"Frrreeeeeeeeeee!" he screamed triumphantly in the morning air, which was still impregnated with the sulfurous vapors of Hell. "Free at last!"

Everything went so fast that Merle scarcely had time to notice any details, not to mention put them together into a logical succession of experiences, pictures, perceptions.

Men were bellowing and running here and there. Soldiers eddied around. Officers shouted orders. Somewhere a shot cracked, followed by a whole hail of bullets. One glanced off Vermithrax's stone flank like a marble, but Merle was not hit.

In a low-level flight, barely nine feet off the ground, the black obsidian lion rushed across the piazza with her. Men parted and ran, screaming. Mothers grabbed their children, whom they'd just let go free after the death of the messenger.

Vermithrax let out a deep growl, like a rockfall in the tunnels of a mine; it was a moment before Merle realized that this was his laugh. He moved with astonishing grace, as if he'd never been imprisoned in the Campanile. His wings were not stiff but powerful and elastic; his eyes not blind but sharp as a hawk's; his legs not lame, his claws not dull, his spirit not dulled.

"He lost the belief in his people," declared the Queen in Merle's thoughts, *"but not the belief in himself."*

"You said he wanted to die."

"That was long ago."

"Live and live and live," roared the obsidian lion, as if he'd heard the words of the Queen.

"Did he hear you?"

"No," said the Queen, *"but he can feel me. And sometimes perhaps even what I am thinking."*

"What *I'm* thinking!"

"What we are thinking."

Vermithrax rushed away over Hell's fissure. The flames were quenched, but a gray wall of smoke divided the piazza like a curtain. Vaguely Merle could see that stone and rubble were filling the crack from below and gradually closing it. Soon only the ruptured pavement would be a sign of the event.

More bullets whistled around Merle's ears, but strangely, during this entire flight she had no fear of being hit. Everything went much too fast.

She looked to the left and saw the three traitors standing in the bunch of guardsmen, in the middle a puddle of slimy secretions that flowed from the body of the messenger.

Purple. Gold. And crimson. The councillors had recognized who was sitting on the back of the lion. And they knew that Merle shared their secret.

She looked forward again, saw the piazza drop behind and the waves rushing under her. The water glowed golden in the dawn, a promising highway to freedom. To their right lay the island of Giudecca, but soon they also left its roofs and towers behind them.

Merle let out a shrill cry, of fear no longer, merely a vent for her euphoria and relief. The cool wind sang in her ears, and finally she could breathe deeply again, a boon after the horrible smell of sulfur in the piazza. Wind stroked her hair, flowed across her eyes, her spirit. She melted with the air, melted too with Vermithrax, who bore her over the sea, forty or fifty feet over waves of liquid fire. Everything was dipped in red and yellow, even she herself. Only Vermithrax's obsidian body remained black as a piece of night that was rushing forward in flight from the light.

"Where are we flying?" Merle struggled to speak over the noise of the wind but wasn't sure she was succeeding.

"Away," cried Vermithrax boisterously. "Away, away, away!"

"*The siege ring,*" the Flowing Queen reminded them. "*Keep in mind the Egyptian heralds and the sunbarks.*"

Merle repeated the words for the lion. Then it occurred to her that Vermithrax had been locked up in the Campanile for so long that he could know nothing of the rise of the Empire and the Pharaoh's war of annihilation.

"There is war," she explained. "The whole world is

at war. Venice is besieged by the armies of the Egyptians."

"Egyptians?" Vermithrax asked in surprise.

"The kingdom of the Pharaoh. He's got a circle around the lagoon. Without a plan we won't get through it."

Vermithrax laughed at the top of his lungs. "But I can fly, little girl!"

"So can the sunbarks of the Empire," retorted Merle, her cheeks reddening. Little girl! Bah!

Vermithrax made a slight turn and looked back over his shoulder. "You make your plan! I'll worry about them back there!"

Merle glanced back and saw that they were being followed by half a dozen flying lions. On their backs sat black figures in leather and steel.

"The Guard! Can you lose them?"

"We'll see."

"Now, don't be reckless!"

Again the lion laughed. "We two will understand each other well, brave Merle."

She had no time to find out whether he was making fun of her. Sharp whistling sounded in her ear—rifle bullets whizzing past them.

"They're shooting at us!"

Their pursuers were about a hundred yards behind them. Six lions, six armed men—no doubt in the service of the traitors.

"Bullets can't hurt me," cried Vermithrax.

"Well, wonderful! Not you, maybe. But they can *me*!"

"I know. That's why we—" He broke off and laughed threateningly. "Here's a surprise for you."

"He's crazy!" If Merle had spoken aloud, her voice would have sounded resigned.

"*Perhaps a little.*"

"Do you think I'm crazy?" asked the lion cheerfully.

Why lie? "You were locked up in that tower for too long. And you know nothing about us people."

"*Did you not reproach me for the same thing?*" the Flowing Queen interjected. "*Do not oversimplify.*"

Vermithrax cut a sharp turn to the right in order to avoid another gun salvo. Merle swayed on his back, but the bushy tip of the lion's tail pressed her firmly into his mane.

"If they keep on shooting so wildly, they'll soon use up their ammunition," she bellowed into the wind.

"*They are only warning shots. They want us alive.*"

"What makes you so sure?"

"*They could have hit us long ago if they had wanted to.*"

"Does Vermithrax know that?"

"*Of course. Do not underestimate his intelligence. These aerial maneuvers are harmless games. He is having fun with it. Possibly he only wants to find out if he has forgotten anything in all the years.*"

Merle's stomach began to feel as if hands were tearing it in different directions. "I feel sick."

"That will pass," replied Vermithrax.

"All right for you to say."

The lion looked back. "There they are."

He'd allowed their pursuers to get closer. Four were just behind them still, but two now flanked them on either side. One of the riders, a white-haired captain of the Guard, looked Merle in the eye. He rode on a quartz lion.

"Give up!" he cried across the gap between them. He was about thirty feet away. "We're armed and outnumber you. If you keep flying in this direction, you'll fall into the Egyptians' hands. We can't allow that—and you can't wish it."

"Which councillor do you serve?" Merle called.

"Councillor Damiani."

"He is not one of the three traitors," said the Queen.

"Why are you following us?"

"I have my orders. And, dammit, that beast under you is the Ancient Traitor, girl! He laid half of Venice to rubble and ashes. You can't expect we'll simply let him go."

Vermithrax turned his head to the captain and inspected him with obsidian eyes. "If you give up and turn around, I'll let you live, human."

Something strange happened. It wasn't the reaction of the guardsman that astounded Merle, but that of his lion. With Vermithrax's words the winged creature awoke from the indifference with which it usually carried out the orders of its human master. The lion stared over at

Vermithrax, and for a long moment its wingbeats became more excited. The captain also noticed this and pulled on the reins in irritation. "Quiet, now." His lips formed the words, but the wind snatched them away.

"The lion cannot understand why Vermithrax talks," declared the Flowing Queen.

"Talk with the lion," cried Merle into the obsidian lion's ear. "That's our chance."

Vermithrax abruptly let himself drop down thirty feet. The length of two men now lay between his paws and the churning sea. The closer they came to the waves, the more keenly Merle perceived their speed.

"Now!" roared Vermithrax. "Hold on tight!"

Merle clutched even deeper in his wind-tossed mane as the obsidian lion speeded up with a series of quick wing-beats, then made a 180-degree turn, climbing at the same time, and suddenly flew at their pursuers.

"Lions," he called over the water in a thundering voice. "Listen to me!"

The six winged lions of the Guard hesitated. The beats of their wings slowed. They hung almost motionless in the air; thus their rumps sank down, moving from the horizontal almost to the vertical. Girths and buckles creaked as the six riders were raised up in their security harnesses. None of them had expected this maneuver. The lions were acting on their own will, and the guardsmen were not used to that.

The captain called out to his men, "Aim at the girl!" But in this position the gigantic heads of their lions were in the soldiers' way, and none of them could aim with only one hand and hold on to the mane with the other.

"Listen to me!" cried Vermithrax once more and looked from one lion to another. He too was floating in place, his wings beating unhurriedly up and down. "Once, I returned to this city in order to free you from the yoke of your oppressors. For a life in freedom. For an existence without compulsion and orders and battles that were never your own. As much air under your wings as you want! Hunting and fighting and, yes, speaking again, when you wish! A life like that of your forefathers!"

"He is using your language," said the Flowing Queen. *"The lions no longer understand their own."*

"They're listening to him."

"You have to ask for how long."

The six riders bellowed helplessly at their lions, but Vermithrax's voice easily overrode theirs. "You hesitate because you have never before heard that a lion speaks the language of men. But do you not also hesitate because there is a lion who is ready to fight for his freedom? Look over at me and ask yourselves: Do you not see in me your own selves again?"

One of the lions spit sharply. Vermithrax started, almost imperceptibly.

"He grieves," explained the Queen. "Because they could be like him and yet they are still only animals."

Other lions joined in the spitting, and the captain, who'd grown up with the lions and spent his entire life with them, smiled with the certainty of victory.

"Rebel against your masters!" Vermithrax bellowed angrily. The mood tipped from one moment to the next without Merle's understanding the reason for it. "Don't take orders anymore! Throw your riders into the sea, or carry them back to the city! But let us go in peace."

The lion that had been the first to spit extended the claws of its front paws threateningly.

"It is no use," said the Flowing Queen with a sigh. "It was worth the try, but it is pointless."

"I don't understand," thought Merle bewilderedly. "Why wouldn't they listen to him?"

"They fear him. They are afraid of his superiority. For many, many years no lion in Venice has spoken. These ones here have grown up in the belief that they are superior to all other lions by means of their wings alone. But now another one comes along who is even more powerful than they. They cannot grasp that."

Merle felt the anger rising in her. "Then they're just like us people."

"Well, well," retorted the Queen. She sounded amused. "Out of the mouths of babes . . ."

"Don't make fun of me."

"No, excuse me. I did not intend to."

Vermithrax spoke softly over his shoulder. "We're going to have to run for it. Get ready."

Merle nodded. Her eyes wandered over the six guardsmen. None of them had yet succeeded in aiming his rifle. But that would change as soon as the lions were horizontal again; as soon as they flew forward again.

"And—go!" roared Vermithrax.

What happened then went so fast that only looking back later did Merle realize how very close to death she had been.

With a roar and powerful wingbeats Vermithrax sped forward, under and past the formation of six guardsmen, steeply up behind them, upside down over them and away.

Merle squealed in horror. Even the Queen cried out.

But Vermithrax turned over and Merle sat right side up again, clutching his mane, still not quite grasping how she'd survived the last seconds safe and sound. The moment during which the sea had suddenly been over her head had been short and not really dangerous— Vermithrax was too fast and had too much momentum for Merle to have been able to lose her grip. Nevertheless . . . he could at least have warned her!

Again they shot over the water's surface, this time toward the south, where the islands of the lagoon were fewer and small in comparison to those up in the north.

Thus they were voluntarily ruling out a whole string of good hiding places, and Merle earnestly hoped that Vermithrax's decision was the right one. He had a plan, she told herself.

"*I do not think so,*" said the Queen demurely.

"You don't?" Merle did not put the question aloud.

"*No. He does not know his way around.*"

"How reassuring."

"*You must tell him what he should do.*"

"I?"

"*Who else?*"

"So you can blame me when we land in Nowhere!"

"*Merle, this affair depends on you, not on Vermithrax. Not even on me. This is your journey.*"

"Without my knowing what we're planning?"

"*You already know that. First: Leave Venice. And then: Find allies against the Empire.*"

"Where?"

"*What happened in the piazza was at least something like a first spark. Perhaps we can get the fire to kindle.*"

Merle made a face. "Could you please express yourself a little more clearly?"

"*The princes of Hell, Merle. They have offered to help us.*"

Merle had the feeling of losing sight of the ground underneath her again, though Vermithrax was flying in a straight line toward the horizon.

"You really intend to ask Hell for help?"

"There is no other way."

"What about the Czarist kingdom? People say they've also stopped the Pharaoh's troops there."

"The Czarist kingdom is under the protection of the Baba Yaga. I do not think it is a good idea to ask a goddess for help."

"The Baba Yaga is a witch, not a goddess."

"In her case that is one and the same, unfortunately."

Before they could get into the subject more deeply, Vermithrax uttered an alarmed shout: "Look out! Now things are going to get unpleasant!"

Merle quickly looked over her shoulder behind them. Between the black feathered wings she saw the open mouth of a lion, and underneath, its outstretched claws. It shot toward them from behind. The target of its attack was not Vermithrax but she herself!

"They wanted it this way," the obsidian lion growled sadly. He whirled around in midflight, so that Merle once again had to hold on with all her might so as not to be thrown from his back. She saw the eyes of the attacking lion widen, an animal reflection of its rider's—then Vermithrax ducked away under the paws of his opponent, turned half to the side, and slit its belly open with a well-aimed blow of his claws. When Merle looked around again, lion and rider had disappeared. The waters of the lagoon turned red.

"They bleed!"

"Just because they are stone does not mean that their insides are any different from those of other living creatures," the Queen said. *"Death is dirty and stinks."*

Quickly Merle turned her eyes away from the red foam on the waves and looked forward, at the outlines of isolated islands approaching. Behind them lay the mainland, a dark stripe on the horizon.

Soon there were two more lions gaining on them. Vermithrax killed the first just as swiftly and mercilessly as his previous opponent. But the other learned from the carelessness of its companion, avoided the slash of the obsidian claws, and tried to reach Vermithrax's underside. Vermithrax cried out as one of the claws grazed him. At the last moment he avoided the deadly blow. Roaring angrily, he flew in an arc, rushed straight at his astonished foe, closer, closer, closer; did not swerve; did not yield; only at the very last second pulled up and swiped the face of the other lion with his rear paws. Stone splintered, then lion and rider disappeared.

Merle felt tears on her cheeks. She didn't want all this death, and still she could not stop it. Vermithrax had urged the lions of the Guard to let them go. Now the only thing left for him was to defend their very lives. He did it with the strength and determination of his people.

"Three left," said the Flowing Queen.

"Must they all die, then?"

"Not if they give up."

"They'll never do that. You know that."

On one of the three surviving lions rode the captain of the Guard. His white hair was tossed by the wind; the expression on his face betrayed uncertainty. It lay on him to order a retreat, but Merle saw by looking at him that he would not even consider that possibility. Capture. If necessary, kill. Those were his orders. For him there was no alternative.

It went fast. Their opponents had not the shadow of a chance. The captain was the only one left, and again Vermithrax bade him retreat. But the soldier only spurred his lion harder. With a lightning move he shot at Merle and Vermithrax. For a brief moment it looked as though the lion of the Guard had in fact succeeded in landing a hit with its claws. But Vermithrax flew an avoidance maneuver that again brought Merle into a dangerous slanting position. At the same time he began the counterattack. The eyes of his enemy showed comprehension, but not even the recognition of defeat was enough to make him turn back. Vermithrax screamed in torment as he dug his claws into the flank of the other; then he turned quickly so that he needn't look as lion and rider plunged into the water.

For a long time no one said a word. Even the Flowing Queen was silent, stricken.

Below them appeared islands with ruins of old fortifications still standing, defenses that people had erected against the Empire. Today they were nothing more than ribs of stone and steel. Cannon barrels rusted in the sun, frosted by the salty winds of the Mediterranean. Here and there forgotten tent poles stuck up out of the swampy wilderness, hardly distinguishable from the three-foot-high reeds.

Once they flew over a section where the water looked lighter, as if a formation of wide sandbanks extended below it.

"*A sunken island,*" said the Queen. "*The currents carried away its walls long ago.*"

"I know it," said Merle. "Sometimes you can still hear its church bells ringing."

But today the ghosts themselves were silent. Merle heard nothing but the wind and the soft rushing of the obsidian wings.

10

SUNBARKS

THE LIGHT OF THE MORNING SUN WASN'T STRONG ENOUGH to brighten the Canal of the Expelled. Its light flowed golden over the upper stories of the houses but ended abruptly twenty-five feet above the ground. Below that, eternal dusk reigned.

The solitary figure hurrying from doorway to doorway was glad of it. He was on the run, and the half-light suited him perfectly.

Serafin stole along the fronts of the empty buildings, continually casting glances behind him to the entrance of the nearest canal. Anyone following him would appear there first, or in the sky above, on a flying lion. However, Serafin thought that was improbable. After everything that had happened in the Piazza San Marco, the Guard presumably had more important things to do—following Merle, for instance.

He'd recognized her on the back of the black beast that had charged out of the tower of the Campanile like a thunderstorm. At first he hadn't believed his eyes, but all at once he was entirely certain: It was Merle, without a doubt. But why was she riding on a winged lion, and moreover, the biggest one Serafin had ever seen? The explanation had to be that it was because of the Flowing Queen. He could only hope that nothing happened to Merle. After all, he was the one who'd gotten them into all this. Why did he always have to stick his nose into things that didn't concern him? If they hadn't followed the lions to the house where the traitors were meeting with the envoy . . . yes, what then? Possibly the galleys of the Pharaoh would already be tied up at the Zattere quay and the canals would be reflecting the annihilating fire from the sunbarks.

In the hubbub and panic in the piazza he'd had no trouble ducking into one of the alleyways. However, it wouldn't be long until the Guard had brought in the information that a former master thief of the Guild was living in the house of Umberto. By afternoon, at the latest, soldiers would be looking for him on the Canal of the Expelled.

Yet where else should he go? Umberto would throw him out if he knew what had happened. But Serafin remembered what Merle had told him about Arcimboldo. Contrasted with Umberto, the mirror maker seemed to be a gentler master—even if Arcimboldo, after all the tricks they'd played on him, probably wouldn't be too happy to speak to a weaver boy. It was a risk that Serafin accepted.

The boat Arcimboldo used once a month to take the new mirrors to their buyers lay tied before the door of the mirror workshop. No one knew exactly who his customers were. But who cared about a few magic mirrors? To Serafin, it all suddenly seemed unimportant.

The front door was standing open. Voices sounded from the inside. Serafin hesitated. He couldn't simply walk in there. If Dario or one of the other boys ran across him on the way, it would be the end of all secrecy. Somehow he must manage to catch the mirror maker alone.

He had an idea. He cast a cautious look at the workshop over on the opposite bank. No one was visible behind the windows. Good. There wasn't a soul in front of Arcimboldo's at the moment either.

Serafin detached himself from the shadows of a doorway and ran. Swiftly he approached the boat. The hull was shallow and elongated. More than a dozen mirrors were hanging in a wooden frame construction at the stern. The narrow spaces between them were padded with cotton blankets.

Other blankets lay in a great heap in the bow. Serafin moved a few to one side, crouched down beneath them, and pulled them over his head. With a little luck no one would notice him. He would make himself known to Arcimboldo when they were under way.

It took a few minutes, but then there were voices. Among them, muffled, he recognized that of Dario. The boys brought a last load of mirrors onto the boat, fastened them securely in the support, and then went back on land. Arcimboldo gave a few instructions, then the boat rocked a bit more strongly, and finally it was under way.

Soon afterward Serafin peered out from under his cover. The mirror maker was standing in the other end of the boat and sculling like a gondolier with an oar in the water. The boat slid unhurriedly down the canal, bent away, went farther. Occasionally Serafin heard the traditional warning calls of the gondoliers crying out before they approached crossings. But most of the time it was utterly silent. Nowhere in the city was it so quiet as in the side canals, deeply embedded in the labyrinth of the melancholy district.

Serafin waited. First of all, he wanted to see where Arcimboldo would land. The gentle rocking was so soothing, it made him sleepy. . . .

Serafin awoke with a start. He'd nodded off. No wonder, under the warm covers and after a night in which he'd never closed an eye. The growling of his stomach had awakened him.

When he looked outside through a gap in the covers, he was more than a little astonished. They'd left the city and were gliding over the open water. Venice lay a great distance behind them. They were heading north, toward a maze of tiny swampy islands. Arcimboldo stood unmoving at the oar and looked out, stony-faced, over the sea.

Now would be a good opportunity. Here outside, no one would see them together. But now Serafin's curiosity won the upper hand. Where was Arcimboldo delivering the mirrors? People no longer lived here since the outbreak of the war; the outer islands were abandoned. Umberto suspected that Arcimboldo sold his mirrors to the rich women of society, the way the master weaver sold his garments. But in this wasteland? They'd even left the lion island far behind them. Only the wind whistled over the gray-brown waves; sometimes a fish could be seen.

Another half hour might have passed before a tiny island appeared. The mirror maker headed for its shore. In the far distance, high over the mainland, Serafin thought he saw small strokes against the sky: the Pharaoh's reconnaissance aircraft, sunbarks, powered by the black magic of the high priests. But they were too far away to be dangerous to their boat. No bark dared venture so deeply into the realm of the Flowing Queen.

The island was about 200 yards across. It was overgrown with reeds and scrubby trees. The wind had pressed tree crowns and knotty branches pitilessly toward the ground. In earlier times such islands had been popular locations for isolated villas erected by noble Venetians. But for more than thirty years no one had come here anymore, never mind lived here. Islands like these were little slivers of no-man's-land, and their mistress was the foaming sea alone.

Ahead of the boat appeared the opening of a small waterway, which wound its way to the interior of the island. On both sides the trees grew densely crowded together, their branches touching the water. Multitudes of birds sat in the branches. Once, when Arcimboldo dipped his oar a bit too forcefully, gulls exploded from the brush and fluttered excitedly over the tips of the trees.

After a last bend, the creek fed into a small lake, which formed the heart of the island. Serafin would have liked to bend forward to see how deep the water was, but it was too risky. Arcimboldo might be sunk in thought, but he certainly wasn't blind.

The mirror maker let the keel of the boat run gently onto land. The hull scraped over the sand. Arcimboldo shipped the oar and went onshore.

Serafin rose up just far enough to see over the railing to the shore. The mirror maker was crouching before a wall of thicket. He drew something in the sand with his index finger. Then he stood up, parted the thicket with his hands, and disappeared into it.

In a flash Serafin shook off the blankets and left the

boat. He made an arc around the strange sign that Arcimboldo's finger had left in the sand and ducked between the plants into damp dusk. He could still see Arcimboldo, a vague shape behind leaves and branches.

After a few more steps he discovered the mirror maker's goal. In a clearing rose the ruins of a building that looked like the pleasure palace of a Venetian nobleman. Only the foundation walls were standing now, darkly black with the burned-on soot of a fiercely hot fire that had left the mansion in rubble and ashes a long time ago. The plant world had long since begun to reconquer its kingdom: Broad fans of vines were climbing over the stones; grass was growing from the jagged tops of walls; a tree leaned out of a window opening like a skeleton with a bony arm outstretched in greeting.

Arcimboldo approached the ruin and disappeared inside. Serafin hesitated, then hurried from his hiding place and took cover behind a wall. Crouching, he stole along it to a burned-out window opening. He carefully raised his head until he could just see over the wall.

The inside of the ruin was an intricate labyrinth of hip-high remains of walls. An unusually large amount of stone was gone, entire walls completely toppled. The old roof tiles formed hills, from which vigorous weeds sprouted. A normal fire would never have been strong enough to cause such destruction. This looked more like the result of an explosion.

Arcimboldo strode through the ruins and kept looking alertly around him. The thought that other people could be stopping at the island made Serafin uneasy. What if they saw him? Possibly they might then leave him marooned here, far away from all the boat routes in the middle of the lagoon.

Arcimboldo bent and again wrote something on the ground with his finger. He turned himself around as he did so, so that the sign in the dust formed a circle. Only then did he right himself again, turning toward the center of the ruin.

"Talamar," he called out.

Serafin didn't recognize the word. It might be a name.

"Talamar!" Arcimboldo repeated. "The wish is fulfilled, the magic worked, the agreement kept." It sounded like a charm, like a magic spell. Serafin was trembling with excitement and curiosity.

Then he noticed the smell of sulfur.

"Talamar!"

The stench was wafting over from the ruin. The source was a place that lay hidden behind the blackened stump of a wall.

There was a hissing sound. Serafin hurried away, along the outer wall, until he came to a window that had a better view of the source of the stench.

It was a hole in the floor, similar to a well. The edge was irregularly mounded up, like that of a crater. This is where the detonation that destroyed the building must have occurred. Serafin couldn't make out how deep the opening was. The hissing grew louder. Something was approaching.

Arcimboldo bowed. "Talamar," he said once more, now a call no longer but a humble greeting.

A spindly creature crept out of the hole on long legs. It was almost human but its joints appeared to bend into wrong angles, which gave it a dislocated, morbid appearance. It moved on all fours—and with its abdomen upward, like a child making a bridge. This made its face upside down. The creature was bald and blind. A wreath of thorny iron tendrils lay close around the eye area like a blindfold. A single spiky loop had escaped and ran crookedly over the face of the creature, straight across the toothless mouth. Where the thorns touched the lips, a broad, bulging scar had formed.

"Mirror Maker," the creature called Talamar whispered, and then repeated Arcimboldo's words: "The wish is fulfilled, the magic worked, the agreement kept. At the service of Darkness forever and ever."

"At the service of Darkness forever and ever," the mirror maker said also. With that, the ceremony of greeting was complete. "I am bringing the order of thirteen mirrors according to the wish of your master."

"He is also yours, Mirror Maker." Despite the unclear speech, the tone of the creature sounded wary. Talamar turned himself with a complicated movement of his angled limbs until his head hung over the edge of the opening. He uttered a string of shrill sounds. In a flash a crowd of black creatures no larger than baby monkeys poured out of the sulfurous shaft. They were blind, like Talamar himself, their eye sockets empty. They bustled hurriedly away. Soon afterward Serafin heard them busy at the boat.

"There's bad news," said Arcimboldo, without stepping outside the circle. "The Flowing Queen has left the lagoon. The water has lost its power. I won't be able to produce any more mirrors until she returns."

"No mirrors?" shrieked Talamar, waving one of his spindly arms. "What are you babbling about, old man?"

Arcimboldo remained calm. No single quiver betrayed any fear or unease. "You understood me, Talamar. Without the Flowing Queen in the waters of the lagoon, I can produce no more magic mirrors. The most important ingredient is missing. That means no more orders." He sighed, his first expression of feeling in the presence of the creature. "Perhaps that won't matter anymore anyway, when the Empire takes possession of the city."

"The masters offered you help," whispered Talamar. "You killed our messenger and turned down our support. You bear the responsibility for this yourselves."

"Not we. Only those who rule over us." Arcimboldo's tone became contemptuous. "Those damned councillors."

"Councillors! Fiddlesticks! All nonsense!" Talamar

gesticulated wildly. The movements made him look still more alien, still more frightening; as always he was standing upside down on all fours. Now Serafin noticed that the creature's heart was beating in a small glass box that was fastened to its stomach with straps—a knotty, black muscle like a pulsating heap of excrement. "Fiddlesticks! Fiddlesticks!" he kept thundering. "Mirrors must be here, more mirrors, more mirrors! So my master wishes."

Arcimboldo frowned. "Tell him that I would gladly do business with him. Lord Light was always a good customer." He said it with a cynical undertone that Serafin understood very well, but Talamar didn't notice at all. "But as long as the Flowing Queen is gone, I can produce no mirrors. Besides, the Egyptians will close my workshop—provided they leave one stone on top of another at all."

Talamar was getting more and more excited, beside himself. "That will not please him. Will not please him at all."

"Do you by any chance fear the anger of your master, Talamar?"

"Fiddlesticks, fiddlesticks! Talamar fears nothing. But you shall fear him, Mirror Maker! You shall fear Talamar! And the anger of Lord Light!"

"I can change nothing about that. I have done business with you so that the workshop would survive. Without your gold I must have closed it long ago. And what would have happened to the children then?" The old man shook his head sadly. "I could not let that happen."

"Children, children, children!" Talamar made a dismissive gesture. But then he distorted his raw lips into a grin. The steel vine over his mouth stretched and pulled the loops over his eyes tighter. "What about the children? You have done everything you were told to do?"

Arcimboldo nodded. "I have taken the two girls into my house, as was the wish of your master." He hesitated. Serafin could see that he was weighing whether to continue, but then he proceeded to keep Merle's disappearance to himself.

Talamar's head swung forward and back. "You have fulfilled all the wishes of the master?"

"Yes."

"And they are also the right girls?"

"All was accomplished to Lord Light's satisfaction."

"How can you know that? You have never met him."

"If it were otherwise, you would have told me, wouldn't you, Talamar?" Arcimboldo grimaced. "It would have been a special joy to you if I were to fall into disfavor with Lord Light."

The creature let out a cackling laugh. "You can supply no more mirrors. The master will be angry." Talamar considered briefly and then a horrible grin split his features. "As recompense we will collect on another contract. Earlier than planned."

Arcimboldo had made every effort to show no weakness before Talamar, but now he could no longer conceal his consternation. "No! It's too early. The plan—"

"Has been changed. Effective immediately."

"That lies outside your authority!"

Talamar neared Arcimboldo until his skinny fingers almost touched the drawn circle. "My authority is Lord Light! You have no right to question it, human! You will obey, nothing else."

Arcimboldo's voice suddenly sounded weak. "You want the girl?"

Talamar giggled. "The girl with the mirror eyes. She belongs to us. You have known that from the beginning."

"But she was supposed to remain with us for years!"

"The change has been initiated. That must be enough. Lord Light will take personal care of her."

"But—"

"Recollect yourself, old man: At the service of Darkness forever and ever! You have sworn an oath. The wish must be fulfilled, the magic worked, the agreement kept. You break the agreement if you supply no more mirrors. For that we take the girl. And remember that sooner or later she would have fallen to us anyway."

"Junipa is only a child!"

"She is the mirror girl. You have made her into that. And as far as the other is concerned—"

"Merle."

"In her there is great strength. A strong will. But not so much power as in the other one. Therefore bring us the mirror girl, old man. Your creature, and soon ours."

Arcimboldo's shoulders sagged. He looked at the ground. He was beaten; defeat was inescapable. Serafin felt pity for him, in spite of all he'd heard.

The column of black monkey creatures returned. Every three bore one of the mirrors over their heads; it looked as though they were carrying fragments of the blue sky over the island. One after the other they marched into the hole, along a path that snaked down the walls of the shaft like a screw thread. Soon not a single mirror could be seen any longer. Arcimboldo and Talamar were again standing alone on the rim of the Hell hole.

"At the service of Darkness forever and ever," yelped the creature.

"Forever," whispered the mirror maker dejectedly.

"I will await you here and receive the mirror girl. She is the most important part of the great plan. Do not disappoint us, old man."

Arcimboldo gave no answer. Silently he watched as Talamar crept back into the hole on his angled limbs, like a human spider. Seconds later he was gone.

The mirror maker picked up the bundle of coins that Talamar had left on the floor and took his leave.

Serafin was waiting for him in the boat.

"You listened to it all?" Arcimboldo was too weak to

show real surprise. Heaviness lay in his movements and his voice. His eyes showed apathy and dejection.

Serafin nodded.

"And—what do you think of me now?"

"You must be a desperate man, Mirror Maker."

"Merle has told me of you. You are a good boy. If you knew the whole truth, you could perhaps understand me."

"Tell it to me."

Arcimboldo hesitated, then he climbed into the boat. "Possibly I shall do that." He went past Serafin, tossed the bag of gold carelessly on the planks, and took up the oar. With tired thrusts he maneuvered the boat along the waterway in the direction of the open sea.

Serafin sat between the empty supports for the mirrors. Small, wet footprints covered the wood.

"Will you do it? Hand over Junipa, I mean?"

"It's the only way. It has to do with much more than my life." He shook his head dejectedly. "The only way," he repeated tonelessly.

"What will you tell Junipa? The truth?"

"That she is a chosen one and always was. Just like Merle—and yet in an entirely different way."

Serafin took a deep breath. "You have truly a lot to tell, Mirror Maker."

Arcimboldo held his gaze for a few seconds longer, then he looked out toward the lagoon, far away, farther still than the landscape, farther than this world.

A gull planted itself on the railing beside Serafin and looked at him with dark eyes.

"It has grown cool," said the mirror maker softly.

After a while Merle thought of the mirror again, the mirror in the pocket of her dress. While she held on to Vermithrax's mane with one hand, she pulled it out of her pocket with the other. It had survived the flight from Venice unharmed. The mirror surface of water gleamed silvery in the late-morning light and sloshed back and forth without a single drop leaving the frame. Once a foggy flicker whizzed across it, only briefly, then was gone again. The phantom. Perhaps a creature from another world, another Venice. What would that look like? Did the people there fear the Pharaoh's kingdom just like the inhabitants of this world? Did sunbarks there also circle in the sky like hungry raptors? And were there also a Merle, a Serafin, and a Flowing Queen there?

"*Perhaps*," said the familiar voice in her head. "*Who knows?*"

"Who, if not you yourself."

"*I am only the lagoon.*"

"You know so much."

"*And yet I possess no knowledge that reaches beyond the boundaries of this world.*"

"Is that true?"

"*Certainly.*"

Vermithrax joined in. His booming voice drowned out the rushing of his wingbeats. "Are you speaking with her? With the Queen?"

"Yes."

"What's she saying?"

"That you are the bravest lion the world has ever seen."

Vermithrax purred like a house cat. "That's mighty nice of her. But you don't have to flatter me, Merle. I owe you my freedom."

"You don't owe me anything at all," she said with a sigh, suddenly downhearted. "Without you I'd probably be dead."

She stuck the water mirror back in her pocket and carefully buttoned it in. A piece of another world, she thought numbly. So close to me. Perhaps Serafin was really right in what he said about the mirror pictures in the canals.

Poor Serafin. What had become of him?

"There ahead!" cried Vermithrax. "Left of us, to the south!"

They had all three known that there would come a moment when they would face the military power of the Pharaoh. Yet so much had happened since they'd left the Campanile, the fears of the siege ring had become distant and diffused for Merle.

But now it had come to the point. In a few moments they would be flying over the ring. It was still a blurry line on the horizon, but it was inching nearer and nearer.

"I'm going to have to climb to a higher altitude," explained Vermithrax. "The air will become thinner, so don't be afraid if you find breathing a little difficult."

"I won't be afraid." Merle tried to give her voice a firm ring.

The gigantic obsidian wings of the lion bore them higher and higher, until the sea beneath them became a uniform surface, without waves, without currents.

Far ahead of them Merle saw the war galleys of the Pharaoh, tiny as toys. The distance could not obscure the fact, however, that the ships had enough destructive power to easily take the insufficient Venetian fleet within hours. The same ships had already—at the beginning of the great mummy war—set loose the first scarab swarms in all the leading countries. The thumb-size eating machines of chitin and malice had rolled inexorably over the continents. First the harvests fell victim to them, then livestock, and finally people. The scarabs were followed by the mummy armies, umpteen thousands snatched from their graves by the high priests of the Pharaoh, furnished with weapons, and sent out to battle, will-less and incapable of feeling pain.

The great war had lasted for thirteen years; then its out-come was decided—as if there'd ever been any doubt about it. The Egyptian Empire had enslaved the people and its armies marched on nearly every street in every part of the earth.

Merle bent deeper over the mane of the stone lion, as if that might protect her from the danger that threatened them from below, from the surface of the sea.

The hulls of the galleys were painted golden, for the indestructible skin of the Egyptian desert gods was also of gold. Each galley had three masts with a multitude of sails. Two rows of long oars projected from the flanks of the hull. In the stern of each ship there was a high construction with an altar on which the high priests in their golden robes performed sacrifices—animals, ordinarily; but also, some whispered, humans.

Small steamboats crossed between the galleys and were used for reconnaissance, provisioning, and pursuit. The siege ring was some fifteen hundred feet wide and extended across the water in both directions to the coasts on either side. There sat diverse arrangements of war machines and foot soldiers, thousands upon thousands of mummy soldiers, who waited, without will of their own, for the signal to attack. It was only a question of days before the Egyptian commanders would receive the final confirmation: Without the Flowing Queen, Venice was helplessly awaiting its downfall.

Merle closed her eyes in despair, before Vermithrax's voice suddenly snatched her from her thoughts. "Are those the flying ships you've spoken of?" He sounded both puzzled and fascinated at the same time.

"Sunbarks," Merle confirmed wryly, as she looked

ahead over the fluttering mane. "Do you think they've discovered us?"

"Doesn't look like it."

Half a dozen slender shapes crossed some distance ahead of them. Vermithrax was flying higher than they were; with a little luck they would pass the barks without the captains noticing them.

The sunbarks of the Empire gleamed golden like the galleys, and since in the sky they were closer than the powerful battleships on the sea, the gleam of their keels was brighter many times over. They were three times as long as a Venetian gondola, roofed over, and provided all around with narrow, horizontal window slits. How many men were behind them was not visible from the outside. Merle estimated that a bark held places for ten people at most: a captain, eight crew members, and the priest whose magic held it in the air. In sunshine the slender flying ships were lightning quick and featherlight to maneuver. When the sky was cloudy, their speed slowed and their movements became clumsy. Finally, by night they were next to unusable.

But on this morning the sun was beaming brightly in the sky. The barks glistened like predators' eyes in front of the hazy background of water and land.

"We'll be over them any minute," said Vermithrax.

Merle's breathing became faster. The obsidian lion had been right: The air up here was thin and caused a pain in her chest. But she said nothing aloud; she was only thankful that Vermithrax was strong enough to take them up so high and over the Egyptians.

"*We have almost made it,*" said the Flowing Queen. She sounded tense.

The sunbarks were now directly under them, glittering blades that soared in wide arcs around the lagoon. No one on board was thinking about the flight of a single lion. The captains were concentrating their attention on the city, not on the airspace above their heads.

Vermithrax sank lower again. Merle felt grateful as her lungs filled more quickly with air. But her eyes were still fixed, spellbound, on the barks, now rapidly falling away behind them.

"Can they see us from the galleys?" she asked hoarsely. No one gave her an answer.

Then they had crossed the ring of warships.

"*Made it!*" the Flowing Queen exulted, and Merle repeated her words.

"It would have been ridiculous not to," growled Vermithrax.

Merle said nothing. But after a while she spoke again. "Didn't you notice anything?"

"What do you mean?" asked the lion.

"How still it was."

"We were flying too high," Vermithrax said. "Sounds don't travel so far."

"*Yes, they do,*" contradicted the Queen, without Vermithrax's being able to hear her. "*You are right, Merle. Complete stillness prevails on the galleys. Deathly stillness.*"

"You mean—"

"*Mummy soldiers. The ships are crewed by living corpses. Just like all the war machines of the Empire. The cemeteries of the conquered lands offer the priests an inexhaustible stock of supplies. The only living men on board are the high priests themselves and the captain.*"

Merle sank into a deep silence. The idea of all those dead who were fighting in the service of the Pharaoh made her even more anxious than the thought of what lay ahead of them.

"Where are we flying?" she asked after a few minutes. They'd gone around the Pharaoh's armies in a large arc and now finally were gliding toward land.

"I'd like to see my homeland again," boomed Vermithrax.

"No!" said the Flowing Queen, and for the first time she availed herself of Merle's voice. "We have another goal, Vermithrax."

The lion's wingbeats became irregular for a moment. "Queen?" he asked uncertainly. "Is that you?"

Merle wanted to say something, but to her horror, the will of the Flowing Queen overcame her own and suppressed her words. With crystalline sharpness it was borne in on her that from now on her body no longer belonged to her alone.

"It is I, Vermithrax. It has been a long time."

"That it has, Queen."

"Will you help me?"

The lion hesitated, then nodded his mighty obsidian head. "That I will."

"Then listen to what I have to say. You too, Merle. My plan affects each one of us."

And then Merle's lips spoke words that were completely foreign to her—places and expressions and over and over a single name: Lord Light.

She didn't understand what it had to do with her, and she wasn't even sure whether at that moment she wanted to know any more about it at all. For the time being nothing could faze her, nothing frighten her. They'd broken through the siege ring, that was all that counted. They'd escaped the grasp of the greatest army the world had ever seen. Merle's relief was so overpowering that all the Flowing Queen's dark prophecies and plans bounced off her as though they had nothing to do with her at all.

Her heart was beating furiously, as if it wanted to burst in her chest, the blood was rushing in her ears, and her eyes were burning from the headwind. Never mind. They'd escaped.

Several times she looked back and saw the rows of galleys and swarms of sunbarks becoming smaller and finally merging entirely into the blue and gray of the horizon— only grains of sand within a world that was too great to look on any longer at all the wrong that the Egyptians had done to it without taking action.

Something was going to happen, Merle could feel that suddenly. Something big, something fantastic. And in a flash came the awareness that this was only the very beginning, mere child's play in comparison to what lay ahead of them.

And then, very gradually it dawned on her that Fate had prepared a special role for her in all of it. She herself and the Flowing Queen, perhaps even Vermithrax.

Although the Queen was still speaking through her, although her lips were moving unstoppably and articulating strange words, Merle permitted herself the luxury of closing her eyes. A rest. Finally. She wanted simply to be alone with herself for a moment. She was almost surprised that she succeeded, in spite of the guest she was harboring.

When she looked again, they had reached the mainland and were flying over scorched fields, bald mountain ranges, and burned villages, and for a long, long time none of them spoke a word.

Lord Light echoed in Merle's thoughts. She hoped the words would provoke the voice inside her to a reaction, an explanation.

But the Flowing Queen was silent.

Merle's fingers curled more deeply into the lion's obsidian mane—something to hold firmly to, a good feeling among so many bad ones.

In the distance they saw the peaks of mountains, far, far away on the horizon. The land stretching to there from the sea had once been full of people, full of life.

But now nothing was living here anymore. Plants, animals, people—nothing.

"They are all dead," said the Flowing Queen softly.

Merle felt the change taking place in Vermithrax even before she stretched out a hand and felt dampness and realized that the obsidian lion was weeping.

"All dead," the Queen whispered.

And then they were silent, looking toward the far peaks ahead of them.